Whatever It Takes

A Center Stage Love Story

Act Three

by

Kathryn R. Biel

Dedication

To Denise.
Thank you for coming into my life and balancing my crazy with your own. Thank you for being a sounding board and also for always having snacks.

Chapter 1: Leslie

Name.

It's the first line on the form. Shouldn't be a hard question. After all, I can still hear my first-grade teacher, Miss Norton, singing, "Name on the paper, first thing" to the tune of "Shave and a Haircut."

Yet here I am, stumped.

I don't want to write it down.

Well, let's get it out of the way. My name is Moose. It's my last name, but still. There it is on *every single document*. Leslie Ann Moose. The worst name ever, with the possible exception of my sister's name—Meredith. Meri Moose is worse but only fractionally more than Les Moose. But she's Doctor Meri Moose, Ph.D., so no one messes with her.

I've heard all the jokes before. Hardy har har. Please don't. Don't even think about it. I don't want to hear it. Now that memes and GIFs are all the rage, I don't want to see it either.

All I want to do is change it.

It's been my dream for as long as I can remember to have a different last name. When I was a small child, I assumed I'd just get married when I was old—like twenty—and the problem would disappear.

Yet here I am at the ripe old age of twenty-six, and marriage isn't even on my radar. One would have to have a second date to get to the marriage point.

Okay, one would have to have a *first date.* But I don't have time for that.

So, I'm going to do the next best thing, which is to take a stage name. It makes sense. I'm a ballet dancer after all. Can you imagine a ballerina named Moose?

It worked so much better for my father, the rugby player, and his father before him. There are already preconceived notions the moment I walk into the room. I don't need my name adding to that.

Maybe that's what's been holding me back all these years.

Probably not, but we can't be too sure, now, can we?

But now I'm staring at the form, the pen frozen in my hand, and I don't know what to write. You'd think I'd have thought of this before now.

I have.

I mean, I've tried. It's just … well, this is my name.

It's me.

For good or bad, I can't come up with anything else. My name has meaning. It was picked for me specifically. I was named after Leslie Caron and Ann

Miller, two iconic dancers. From the moment of my birth, I was destined to be a dancer.

And now here I am, at a musical theater audition. The stars fated this upon me.

"Last call for applications! Turn them in now!" the production assistant yells.

Without thinking, I hand the application to her. It's not until after she disappears behind the double doors that I realize I never actually put a name on it.

Great.

I've already failed, and I haven't even started.

It's too late now. I'm herded into a large dance studio with about fifteen other females. I look around at my competition. We're all wearing black leotards, as is standard for ballerinas. This may be a musical theater audition, but we're all ballerinas at the core, as this role requires. I've eschewed the traditional pale pink tights and shoes for ones that better match my brown complexion—anything to lengthen my curvy lines.

It's not unusual that I'm the only brown one in the room. That's how it was in dance class, growing up in the suburbs of Columbus, Ohio. There was a bit more diversity at the Five Boroughs Ballet Company, where, up until recently, I'd spent all my time as a trainee. *Nope, can't think about that situation. I've got a job to do. I've got to be my best right now.*

After about thirty minutes of barre warm-up, the choreographer introduces herself as Kori, and without much fanfare, begins to teach us the combo. One minute doesn't sound like a long time until you're trying to commit a dance sequence to memory. It's not like I don't do this every day.

At least I used to.

I haven't danced in six weeks.

The last time I went this long without attending a ballet class was the summer I was sixteen and the doctors suggested I take the summer off from dance. From ballet at least. Instead, my parents sent me to drama camp.

If you can't dance, you can at least continue developing your expression and stage presence. There are a lot of skills you can still work on.

Who knew that I'd be pulling from lessons learned at that camp now?

The combination is not that hard. It's far from the most challenging thing I've ever danced. I mean, that's why I'm here right? That's why I'm giving up and selling out. Still, my knee twinges, threatening to pop, and my toenails are too long.

And then I wait for my number to be called.

"Number seventy-two!" the production assistant bellows.

It's go time.

The director isn't even paying attention. I wait, clutching my résumé and headshot.

"And?" he asks.

I don't know what he's looking for. He sighs and rolls his eyes. I swallow hard. "I'm sorry about the info form."

"Doesn't bode well for you."

Oh shit. Have I already blown it? If he'd just let me ex—

He cuts me off, barking, "Do you have a name?"

What an asshole. I don't know if I even want to work for this dude.

On the other hand, I do want to eat and pay rent.

I stutter out, "Um yes, but I'm considering starting to use a stage name. I can't decide."

Honesty is the best policy.

The asshole rolls his eyes. Maybe honesty is not the best policy. Maybe I should have told him that I transcend traditional identifications of arbitrary names thrust upon us by a patriarchal society.

"Okay, are you ready?" he asks.

I nod and the production assistant cues the music. As it begins, the director's phone pings, pulling his attention.

Do not let this bother you. Do your best. Be the best. Whatever it takes. Dance as if your next meal depends on it.

Because it does.

Smile, look wistful, and be endearing. Look innocent. Hope that I don't look twenty-six, considering Lise is supposed to be a teenager. Channel my inner Leslie Caron, my namesake, who originated the role in *An American in Paris* in 1951.

Walk one two, run run rond de jambe. Delicate hands. Snap on the fouetté arabesque. Shoulders down. Look wistful. Reach three four, port de bras.

As I finish down on my knee, I ignore the pain and wait. Finally, the director says, "That's great. Thanks."

There's no way to read anything into that.

I stand, hold my head up high, and walk toward the door. Out in the hall, I remove my bronze Gaynor

Minden pointe shoes, pulling back my convertible tights to reveal the blisters that have formed after only ninety short minutes.

No pain, no gain.

I pull a loose dress on over my leotard and tights, sliding my feet into my beat-up, cozy Uggs. I look up and down at the rest of the ballerinas in the hall. I wonder how many they'll call back. When will we hear? I yank my phone out of my bag and check the time. I've got a shift at the diner in two hours. I can't afford to miss it.

The door opens again and the production assistant steps out. "Okay, we need numbers fifty-five, fifty-nine, sixty-seven, and seventy-two to stay for vocal auditions. Everyone else, thank you."

A flood of relief washes through me. I made it through to the next round. I haven't failed. Not yet.

I'll ignore the small fact that being here in the first place is a failure. I push that thought way down deep. Now I have to sing.

I pull out my sheet music, humming the tune in my head. My audition piece has remained "On My Own" from *Les Mis* since I worked on it that summer at camp. It's the piece I know best, so it's like coming home to visit an old friend when I sing it.

And it makes me think of an old friend. One whom I wasn't much of a friend to.

I'll be the last one to go since I have the highest number. I set my music down on the floor next to me and pull out my phone again. I should probably look this theater company up. I don't really know anything about them, other than they're north of the city.

Oh God, they're like two hours north of Manhattan in someplace called Hicklam. It even sounds like it's the end of the earth.

Shit.

How'm I gonna manage that? I can't commute there every day. And it's not like I can afford two places. I can barely afford my share of the rent right now. My parents still send me money for shoes, which I haven't needed, so I've been relying on that to augment.

Another problem to figure out. Who knew being a failure was so time consuming?

Before I can fully fall down this shame spiral, a name catches my eye.

Josh deChambeau, Musical Director.

I gasp, my breath involuntarily leaving my body as a wave of emotion crashes into me. It was like thinking of him conjured him back into my life.

Josh.

His smile instantly pops into my mind. God, I need to see it again. If I get this part, I'll get to see Josh. I'll get to work with him again. I'll get to apologize—finally—for what I did.

The pressure has just leveled up.

No matter what, I *have* to get this part.

I did not get the part.

"Yeah, but you're the understudy. That's at least something," Imani offers cheerfully. "It's a paying job. And you know you'll get stage time. It's really great. You should be pumped."

I know my roommate is only trying to help. She's always trying to help. She doesn't understand the whirling vortex of thoughts inside my brain.

Hell, I don't even understand them most of the time.

"The pay is shit."

"You're a performing artist. The pay is always shit. But you can sublet here and save that money, so that's something. I bet my cousin Jade would take it. And you know she won't trash the place."

"Not really. It's only about four weeks. Not long enough to sublet."

"I bet I can talk Jade into something. Maybe she'll want to move in here permanently, so we can cut the rent down some more."

There's already two of us in a studio. I don't think I can handle one more.

Of course, there's not much I can handle right now.

"Are you going to tell your parents?"

I sigh. It's the question I've been grappling with for the past seven weeks since the day I was officially let go from the Five Boroughs Ballet Company. It shouldn't be a shock to them. The writing's been on the wall for several years.

On the other hand, it was still a shock to me. Part of me truly believed that if I showed up every day and worked and sweated and bled for my craft then it would be enough to be successful.

I'm twenty-six and only made it into the corps de ballet at the age of twenty-five because of a freak accident that put six members of the corps on the injured list in the middle of last season.

I didn't make it because I was good enough. I only made it because they were desperate.

Still, I really thought they'd see my potential; that I was worthy of a spot permanently. Or at least for one more season. But before you could say plié, there I was, in Roberto's office, with him telling me what a *pleasure* it'd been to work with me and how they were *eternally grateful* that I'd been able to fill in in a pinch. But I had to understand that I'd outlasted the normal *time frame* of a trainee.

And then he sent me on my way.

I don't even get to take classes there anymore. My temporary corps status has been revoked. I'm no longer considered a trainee. Apparently, I'm not trainable.

Ballet is now recreation for me. I can't even call myself a ballerina anymore.

Auditioning for this part at The Edison was a last-ditch effort to stay professional. To stay relevant. To prove that I wasn't a total failure.

God, I can't believe how far I've let myself fall. I've always wanted to do my best. To be the best. And now I'm settling for barely not failing.

Yeah, no. I won't be telling my parents about this. I don't even have to hear their voices to know what their disappointment will sound like.

"Not right now."

"But won't they want to fly in from Columbus to see you? They did when you were in *Giselle*."

I shrug, trying to ignore the sick feeling creeping up from my stomach. Instead, I focus on the laundry I'm folding.

How can I even invite my parents out? There's no guarantee that I'll ever even perform. It'd be like going to my dad's rugby game, only to have him never join the scrum.

It goes without saying that even with injuries, he always played. Started. Because that's what you do when you're the son of the best rugby player in Fijian history. You topple your father's records and become the new best.

Each generation shall be better than the last. We will be the best. Whatever it takes.

Except taking a role in a stage production of a ballet, instead of performing in an actual ballet, is not the best. Especially when that role is the understudy. It might be better to walk away than to admit that I'm second rate.

"I don't know, it's like I'm selling out."

"Again, you're a performing artist. Everything you do is selling out. You do it so you can do your craft. Don't you want to get paid to dance? Don't you want the chance to perform? You aren't guaranteed any more chances if you don't take it." Imani looks around our tiny apartment, her gaze landing on the poster above my bed. She smirks. "You're obsessed with this show. I'd never even heard of *An American in Paris* until I met you. Weren't you like, named after it?"

14

I look at the poster from the Broadway musical adaptation, cartoon Lise's yellow dress ruffling in the Paris breeze. "I was named after the actress who played her in the movie."

"So you were like, literally born for this role." Imani picks up a pair of socks I've just meticulously rolled and tucked. "You'd be stupid not to take it." She throws the socks at me. I attempt to catch them but miss, just as I did with every ball ever tossed my way, much to the chagrin of my athletic father and grandfather.

I plop down on the couch and pull out my phone. For the second—okay, seventeenth—time, I pull up the website for The Edison, clicking on the link for musical director Josh deChambeau.

His hair is much longer than it was ten years ago. It now hangs in flowing wavy locks to his shoulders if his headshot is still accurate. Behind the scenes photos show him sitting at a piano, dressed in black. But there's this one picture that I can't tear my eyes away from. It's from some casual performance. Josh is perched on a stool, hunched over his guitar. He's wearing old jeans and a T-shirt with the sleeves ripped off. His hair, pulled back, is escaping from the band, and pieces fall around his face. That's not what gets me. It's his smile, white teeth all in a row.

The same smile that broke through the world of pain I was in and touched my soul.

It's familiar and comforting, and it soothes me like a tonic.

Ten years ago, I fell in love with that smile. Ten years later, I'm even more broken than I was then.

But he saw me through my faults and loved me anyway.

Maybe I just need someone to love me again, despite my shortcomings.

Aww, hell.

I'm going to Hicklam.

Chapter 2: Josh

Josh, man, you're the luckiest son of a bitch I've ever met."

While I appreciate D'von's words of encouragement, I don't know that my drummer has the best perspective on my life. What he sees might seem like luck, but there's been a tremendous amount of *suck* along the way.

Not to mention hard work. To me, luck would be a lot easier.

"How so now?" I flex my fingers over the keyboard of the baby grand, getting ready to warm up for our gig. I run up and down doing some scales.

"You're heading back to The Edison next week, right?"

I nod, now plinking out the melody running through my head. It's been haunting me night and day. I've got to write it down soon so I can work on the lyrics to match. I scribble the notes on the back of the music we're using tonight, before replacing the paper on the piano. Now I just have to remember later that I did this and where I put it. My dad was forever writing down music and leaving it here and there. When my sister and I cleaned out the house, we found enough scraps of paper with indecipherable notes to fill a bookshelf.

I'm at least going to be organized about my indecipherable notes.

"This season is going to be lit. You're so lucky. You've got to get me tickets. I want to go on tour with them. Maybe you can get us in as their permanent backup band if they're doing another reunion. That would be dope."

His words rain down on me, not quite connected and definitely not making any sense. I need to pay more attention. "Say what now? What are you babbling about?"

"Tabby Cat."

I squint, trying to figure out what a cat has to do with me at The Edison. I mean, sometimes there are strays who wander around the property, but that really has nothing to do with anything. "Huh?"

He pulls out his phone and after a few taps, shoves it under my nose. "See? Tabby Cat is doing a show at The Edison. You *have* to get us booked as the Sassy Cats backup band. Or at least me."

I scan through the article. "This is new." Grayson and Henderson never mentioned anything about it during our last team meeting. "Whatever. As long as she shows up. That's all I care about."

"You know she's like best friends with Angie Aliberti. And Mandy Calhoun too."

I stand up from the piano bench and clap my friend on the back. "I'm so proud that you know who the Sassy Cats are. Did you have their posters hanging in your room too? But why do I care about who she's friends with? It doesn't affect me in any way. I'm pretty sure she's not going to be asking who my drummer is and if we paint each other's nails every weekend."

D'von rolls his eyes. "Man, you gotta think outside the box. She's a legit star who has other legit stars as her friends. And they all have money. As in, money to produce your show … if you ever finish it."

Well, damn. D'von's got a point. I've only been working on this damn show for five years now.

"Hell, isn't that why we play all these stuffy Manhattan events? So you can get hooked up with these swanky rich people and someone will bankroll you?"

"More so that I can eat and pay rent. Not to mention play. None of it's worth doing if I can't play." I run my fingers up the ivory keys in a glissando.

D'von punctuates my statement on his set with a sting, the ba dum tss echoing through the marble banquet room. "Damn straight, bro. Damn straight."

"Hey, Josh. D'von. Sorry, I'm late." Mei bustles in with Mark, the bass player, close on her heels.

"Yeah, Mei and I ended up on the same train," Mark supplies, though neither one of us asked him.

"I mean, we're coming from the same area of SoHo, so it's not that unusual." She shrugs out of her long black coat and tosses it over the amp. She straightens and flips her long ebony hair over her shoulder. She smooths her fitted black gown over her narrow hips. "Does this look okay?" Mei turns in a slow circle for me.

I stand up, appreciating the view. "You shouldn't have worn that." Her face falls. *Oh shit*. Quickly, I correct. "Because no one's going to be looking at the bride."

"Yeah, Mei. You're smoking hot. I mean, you could always show a little more up top, but this is good. Just turn around a lot so people can see that fine ass."

It's a wonder Mark doesn't have a girlfriend. Mei glares at him.

I lean in and give her a quick peck on the lips. "You look beautiful, as always. Do you want to do some vocal warm-ups before the guests start arriving?" I look at my watch. We're due to start in about fifteen minutes. Mei and Mark were really cutting it close.

Good thing D'von and I were here with plenty of time to set up and get changed. If I didn't know better, I'd think Mark was late simply to avoid moving the gear. Since this ballroom has its own baby grand, I didn't have to haul my keyboard in. I'd much rather play on an actual piano any day.

Mark finally unpacks his bass and begins warming up. We only have a minute or so to tune before the frazzled-looking wedding planner's assistant comes rushing in. The wedding planners themselves never appear frazzled, but their poor staff are often sweating heavier than professional athletes in a sauna.

I smile as I sit down at the piano, ready to spend the next three hours serenading guests while they sip their top-shelf cocktails and snack on the fanciest hors d'oeuvres I've ever seen. There's another band coming in for after dinner. We get the first dance. They get the drunken fun.

Sometimes I watch the bride and groom, trying to see if they're really in love. Do they believe in it at all, or is all of this for show? Generally speaking, the fancier the wedding, the less true love there seems to be.

Maybe I'm wrong. Maybe I'm a cynic. Maybe they already know that love can be vicious. I glance over at Mei, singing Sinatra with her throaty voice. Maybe love deserves a second chance.

Still, the pay is good. If I wanted this hustle year-round, I could probably make out better than I do working for The Edison. However, my goal in life is not to be a jazz pianist playing gigs every weekend.

I've got plans. I've had them for as long as I can remember. And nothing's going to stand in my way of achieving them.

It's why I've been working so hard on composing and writing my own show. If I have my way, my name'll be up there with Stephen Sondheim and Lin Manuel Miranda. So I pay my dues at The Edison and pay my bills with fancy gigs. It's a balance I hope I don't have to maintain forever.

By the time we get the gear loaded up in D'von's van, it's almost midnight. Tuxedo bag slung over my shoulder, I approach Mei. "Are you coming back to my place tonight?" She usually does after gigs, both of us too wired to sleep right away.

Might as well pass the time together.

"I didn't bring a change of clothes, so we'll have to go to my place."

I hate going to her place. Her roommates are loud and annoying. Plus I was sort of hoping to work on my show once Mei fell asleep. I do some of my best composing as I'm trying to doze off, and I don't have my notebook to write anything down in.

"Fine."

She wrinkles her nose. "Don't sound so excited about it. You don't have to come over. I'm pretty sure I'll live without you tonight."

I step back and look at her. She's stunning. Her voice is smooth and sultry. But other than that, I'm not sure what's really there between us, other than the physical.

"I think I'll just go home. I need to work on my show."

She rolls her eyes. "Right. The show."

"It's coming together. I have the end of Act One and the ballad left to write, and I got some of that down earlier tonight while we were waiting for you." I pat my pocket, where I've folded up the sheet music so I don't lose my creation. "Once I can get this done, I'll be able to focus more on … other things," I finish lamely.

"I've heard that before. Fine. You don't want to come home with me, don't. It's your loss." She turns on her heel, storming toward the door.

I shake my head and pull out my phone to get an Uber. It's too late and I'm too tired to worry about taking the subway to my Brooklyn apartment. Plus,

I've got five hundred bucks in cash burning a hole in my pocket, tempting me to live a little dangerously.

It's probably better for me when I get Venmo'd the money. At least that way, I'm less inclined to spend it right away.

My phone alerts me that my car is approaching, so I head out into the cold March night. Spring is threatening to thaw us out, but she's certainly taking her own sweet time getting here. As I exit the building, I see a flash of Mei's leg as she climbs into the back of her own ride. The sedan pulls away from the curb, and I swear I see another body in the back with her. God, I hate it when she UberPools. You never know what kind of person you'll be sharing a car with.

Damn, I should have bitten the bullet and gone back to her place. On the other hand, this show isn't going to write itself. I'd always hoped that maybe Grayson would offer to do the show at The Edison, at least to start off. But now I see that D'von is right. Tabby Cat may be the shot I need.

I've got to get this done.

I hum out the tune I'd been working on earlier as I change into sweats and a faded T-shirt. It's only after I'm dressed do I realize what I'm wearing. Most people would assume the "STP" logo is for the band, Stone Temple Pilots, but I know it stands for Stagehands Theatre Productions.

It's the theater camp that changed my life.

It showed me what I wanted in life. I'd always known music was what I wanted, but until those eight weeks in the Catskill Mountains, I didn't know exactly how I'd want to pursue that career. Prior to that, I'd only been part of the pit band when the school was desperate. I'd never actually considered theater. That summer changed everything.

In fact, it was then, ten years ago, that I first came up with the idea for my show. It was *her* assigned summer reading, so we spent countless hours acting it out with each other.

That was my first mistake.

Falling in love with her was my second.

I shake my head, desperate to clear those memories. No, I need to focus. It's the ballad. The one the show will be known for.

I've got to get this right. I'm sure there's some deep-seated message here about how I've spent the past five years writing a musical to a play we read together five years before that. A show about betrayal and lying.

And love.

Chapter 3: Leslie

Three Months Later

L eslie, it's Mom. Not sure what you're up to. Call me back."

I don't know why my mom insists on leaving a message every single time she calls. I always call her back as soon as I'm able. Probably because Mom and Dad drilled into Meri and me from the time we had cell phones that if we didn't answer or didn't call back within a few minutes, we lost our phones.

I may still harbor an irrational fear about having my phone taken away.

I'm listening to her message while on the train home. I just got off my shift, and it's too late to call her back now, even though she called around three. It'll have to wait until tomorrow. I shoot her a text, telling her that. I've been picking up the late-night shift a lot, finding that drunk people tend to be a little more generous with their tips. There are fewer drunk people on a Monday night, but still, the tips were decent tonight. I'm making ends meet—for now—just working a mere sixty to seventy hours a week on my feet.

It only leaves me time to take a few hours of ballet class—recreational, of course—which is the least I've ever danced since I was six, if you don't count that summer I did theater camp.

It's one of those interesting situations. Ballet has definitely broken my brain, but on the other hand, my brain only feels right when I'm dancing. An hour of class here and there isn't quite enough to keep me feeling good.

I'm almost wondering if I'd be better off walking away from ballet altogether. I've never actually considered doing that before, but it would make sense. Whether I'm ready to face it or not, I'm not going to have a career as a professional ballerina.

I'm like Moonlight Graham in *Field of Dreams*, who made it to the major leagues but never got to bat. Except I'm in satin pointe shoes.

I doubt Kevin Costner will be building me a stage in the middle of a cornfield any time soon so I can achieve my dreams.

One can hope though.

Most people get a lifetime of working toward their apex. I had to go and pick a career with a limited shelf life and early retirement age. Hell, even if I'd become a principal dancer, I'd probably be done by the age of thirty-five or so. But if that were the case, then I'd have achieved my goals and been the best, and there would be no shame in moving on to the next great thing to conquer. Just like my father, and his father before him, who both pitched their way to world championships with the Fiji Sevens National Rugby team.

At fifty-three, my dad now coaches in a successful high school program, taking part in molding the next generation of ruggers—as I like to call them—into successes. Though I doubt any of the mid-Western Ohio boys he coaches will ever come near winning Olympic gold medals like the Fiji National Team did in both the 2016 and 2020 Olympics. Go Flying Fijians!

He's not only had one successful career but two. All while being a doting husband and loving father.

I can barely pay my rent, and I was stood up by a Tinder date last week.

I'm not gonna lie, it's getting hard to look in the mirror. The only thing worse would be having to face my parents.

Which is why seeing them both standing impatiently outside my apartment when I walk down the street is rather disconcerting. Not to mention it's after one a.m.

"Mom! Dad! What are you doing here? I got your message, but I worked a double and just got off. It was too late to call you back. I was going to call in the morning. I swear. I texted you. You didn't have to come all the way out here."

Wait, why are they here? Columbus is a good fifteen-hour drive.

"When you find out your daughter's life is completely off the rails and she's been hiding it from you, you take the first flight." My mom crosses her arms over her chest.

KATHRYN R. BIEL

Shit.

So my dad is a 6'4" hulking, muscle-filled, dark-skinned Fijian who has made a career out of creaming other hulking, muscle-filled men on the field. Yet my Irish-German mother, who topped off at about 5'2", is the more intimidating of the two.

She's in full-on silent rage mode, which is the most terrifying of her emotions. I'd rather have her screaming like a lunatic. The calmness of her voice instantly has me wanting to break down in tears.

Instead, I do what I've always done when I can't face the disappointment I know I'm causing. I lie.

"I'm not off the rails. I'm totally good. Great. I just decided to pick up some more shifts for a little extra money. No big deal. I'm fine."

"Fine. We've heard that one before."

I'd like to roll my eyes, but I don't dare. I may be twenty-six, but you just don't do that with Mama Moose. I'll never be old enough to roll my eyes at my mother.

"Um, should we go in?" my dad suggests.

"I'm not sure if Imani's there or not," I stall. I can't help but notice he's wearing the Moose family T-shirt. The one that says, "Do your best. Be the best. Whatever It Takes." I'm not sure exactly when the Avengers started using that phrase, but it's been the Moose family creed my entire life. We've had several versions of these shirts made over the years.

Needless to say, I am not the best.

"Why don't you come back to the hotel with us then? We have some things to discuss." My dad may have phrased it in the form of a question, but there's

28

only one acceptable answer. At least they're not planning on crashing with me. That would be terrible. No room to get away from them and their probing questions about the disastrous path my life has taken.

"Okay, great. Let me just run up and grab a change of clothes. I smell like grease."

"Did you at least eat something when you got off work?"

This time, I do actually sigh. At least I mentally sigh. "Yes, Mother. I ate. A sandwich."

I should tell her that I had a half—okay a quarter of—a turkey club sandwich, but I'm sick of accounting for my food. Her worry is not without good cause. I don't know if she'll ever believe that I've moved on from that stage in my life.

On the other hand, now that I'm not dancing as much, I can't afford to eat as many calories in a day. It's a delicate balance.

After packing a quick bag and leaving a note for Imani, I rush back down the stairs to find my parents waiting in a rental car. I slide wordlessly into the back seat and begin counting. I only make it to fourteen before the onslaught begins.

"Do you want to explain what you've been doing with yourself?" My mom doesn't say "young lady," but her tone implies it. I catch my dad's concerned gaze in the rearview mirror.

Sometimes he's my ally. I'm not sure if this is one of those times.

"Oh you know, taking classes. Working. Living the dream. Same old, same old."

"Really? Because you're no longer listed on the Five Boroughs Ballet Company website."

Whomp, there it is.

I sit in the back seat of the car, looking at my hands in my lap. Shame flames my cheeks. It's bad enough to have been fired. It's worse to know I disappointed my parents.

Again.

I twist my fingers, picking at the errant cuticle on my index finger. "Yes, well, you know I was only promoted to corps because of that accident." I shrug, even though they can't see it. "Everyone's better now. They didn't need me."

My mom whips around, her pale fingers gripping the back of the seat. "But you were supposed to use that opportunity to prove yourself!"

My voice rises to meet hers. "I tried, Mom. I really did. I was there day in and day out. Longer than was required. I danced until my feet bled, and then I danced some more. But let's face it, I'm not good."

Against my will—as are so many things in my life right now—the tears I've been attempting to suppress escape and run down my cheeks. My parents hate it when I cry. I hate it when I cry. It's like announcing to the world that I'm a baby who can't deal with anything.

"There's no need to cry. And you know you're good. I don't know why you would say you're not."

With the back of my hand, I slash the tears away from my face. "Well, of course, I'm good. I wouldn't have made it this far if I wasn't. I'm just not good enough to be a professional ballerina."

The statistics don't lie. Only about two percent of training ballerinas make it into a top professional company. I'm in the other 98th percent. Realistically, I was probably in the top four percent. It was close, but not close enough.

My mom takes a deep breath in. My dad still says nothing. This is pretty standard for them. He may be big and strong, but when it comes to parenting and emotions and, well, anything difficult, Mom does all the heavy lifting.

"Do you think it's because of ..." she trails off, tipping her head toward Dad.

"No, I don't. Not here at least." Her concern is valid. It was definitely an issue in Ohio, but not at FBBC. New York is more progressive than the Midwest. "I think it's because I'm not as technically skilled. You know my posture's always been an issue. I'm not a great turner. My jumps are too athletic-looking."

My stature, at 5'6", is more like the compact muscular builds of gymnasts than the long, lean, waif structure normally associated with ballerinas. And then there's my full D's. No matter what, they bounce when I dance. I'm a great jumper though, with solid thigh muscles.

That's not what the traditional ballet world wants to see.

As the car pulls into the harshly-lit parking garage, I can see how crestfallen my mother is.

I see her disappointment and raise her one.

We get out of the car and my dad slings his big arm over my shoulders. "Tough break, kiddo. No worries, though. We'll make sure your room's ready as soon as you can get out of your lease."

I stop walking. "Wait, what?"

My mom turns around, adjusting her large pink purse on her shoulder. "What?"

"I'm not breaking my lease."

"Of course you are. You're coming home. There's no need for you to be here anymore."

"Other than I live in New York. There's like, literally *nothing* for me back in Ohio." Not to mention no way in hell am I going back there, tail between my legs.

"There's not much here for you either," Dad says. Oh shit, if he's weighing in, it's gettin' serious. I'm going to lose this argument. Time to pull out the big guns.

"Actually, I'm not totally done. I'm just pivoting."

I hate that expression.

By this time, we've reached the hotel lobby. We're silent as we step into the elevator. At this late hour, there's no one around.

"What do you mean by pivoting? And don't be a smart-ass and tell me it's some kind of turn." My mom is done being patient.

"I, um, well, I have a role in a musical theater production. It runs for two weeks. The theater's here, in New York." I casually omit that it's in New York State, not New York City. That's a distinction I don't really want to make right now. The same goes for the fact that I'm the understudy, not the lead. "I start rehearsals in a few weeks. I have to be there for that.

And the best part? It's *An American in Paris*." I lay my trump card down with a flourish.

My mom's face lights up, beaming with pride. "Oh, I knew it. I'm glad you didn't give up. And you were born to be Lise!"

Gotta love how she automatically assumes I have the lead rather than the ensemble.

"We didn't raise her to give up. Or to accept second place. She's going to be the best. Whatever it takes." Dad's strong hand claps down on my shoulder.

I can barely sleep in the hotel. Partially because of Dad's tympanic snoring, but mostly because of the guilt eating me from the inside out.

I should have told them the truth.

Honesty is the best policy.

Sure, it is, except when being honest hurts them. And me.

I'm not sure I've slept for more than a few hours when I'm woken by the sound of my phone. It's The Edison. Oh please God, don't be firing me.

"Leslie Ann Moose?"

I should have come up with a stage name. "Yes?"

"It's Henderson Quade from The Edison." I recognize his Australian accent. "We're in a bit of a pickle, and we're wondering if you'd be able to step into a role."

"You want me to do a role? In addition to the one I auditioned for?"

My conversation has piqued the interest of both my parents. My mom begins jumping up and down and asking questions. I wave my hand in a desperate effort to silence her.

"Yes. It's the role of Anne Wheeler in *The Greatest Showman*. You know, the one Zendaya played in the movie."

"The trapeze artist?" Oh shit. I don't know how to trapeze. Or whatever it's called.

"Yes. We were thinking that with your strong dance background, we'd be able to figure something out. The lodging would begin now, and you'd receive full salary for your time."

This is too good to be true. "What's the catch?"

"The show opens July first. Today is already day three of rehearsals."

I glance at my watch to see the date. It's June sixteenth. "It's not a lot of time."

"No, and we're opening this show a day earlier than normal. You only have two weeks to learn everything."

Including a brand new skill that I don't actually possess.

And a singing skill that's not so great itself. At least not without a lot of work.

My mom's nodding her head so vigorously that she's going to give herself a headache from her brain rattling around in there. She doesn't know that this guy was an ass during auditions and that he cast me as the understudy. But *now* I'm good enough.

Once again, I wasn't the best. I was the runner-up.

I know I'm going to take this part because it sure beats the alternative of going back to Ohio, but he doesn't need to know that.

"I can come up today and look around. I can't commit beyond that without fully assessing the situation." I wink at my dad. This is one of his tactics. "What's the best way to get there? Train?"

I'm sure my parents would offer to drive me, but there's no way in hell I'm letting them anywhere near The Edison. That has disaster written all over it.

"Yes. Let me know what time you're due to arrive, and we'll have someone pick you up. Do you want me to email you the script or music or anything?"

"Why not. I'm not sure if I'll have time to look at it before I get there, but it can't hurt."

I disconnect and now it's my turn to jump up and down, clapping my hands. "I'm gonna be a star!"

Chapter 4: Josh

I've never been in a better mood. Tabitha threw an epic party at her place last night. It was seriously the coolest thing I've ever been to.

Mostly because I got to throw back a few beers and chill with Ben Reynolds. You know, Grammy-winning songwriter Ben Reynolds. I *may* have even pitched my show idea to Ben and his girlfriend, Mandy Calhoun.

They didn't hate it.

Ben was actually quite interested and told me to get in touch when it's done. I'm like 95 percent of the way there. That last ballad, "Purple Dawn," still isn't quite right. Meaning, other than the title, I don't have much.

I'm not sure if they'll actually listen to anything when the time comes, but they didn't say no. That's a huge hurdle, and I just sailed over it with room to spare.

I wish I could call my parents to tell them. There are so many times I wish I could pick up the phone and talk to them. They'd both be so happy. Instead, I shoot a text to my sister, Kim, who probably couldn't care less. An actuary, she didn't inherit my parents' musical genes. Still, she's supportive, sending me back a thumbs-up emoji.

"Hey, man, we need a favor." Grayson looks like crap. It's too early in the rehearsal process for things to be falling apart, but nevertheless, here we are. I may have had a great night, but it didn't end so well when Jasmine sliced through her hand trying to shuck an oyster.

I don't know what she was thinking, other than I'm fairly sure she was lit and those knives are super sharp.

It doesn't matter what she was thinking though, because I don't know how she's going to perform her role as Anne in *The Greatest Showman*. Jasmine is an aerial artist, and she and Levi have been working hard on their "Rewrite the Stars" number. It has the potential to be a showstopper. *Had*. There's no way in hell Jas is going to be able to do any of that aerial work with a damaged hand.

I don't even hesitate. "Anything."

"Okay, so we've got someone coming in from the city to possibly take Jasmine's role. She's the understudy for another role for us later this summer, but she's undecided about this part and needs a little coaxing. Okay, a lot of coaxing. We don't have any other options if she refuses. I'm knee-deep in rehearsals and Henderson, well ..."

"Say no more. Henderson's great at a lot of things, but schmoozing isn't exactly his forte."

Grayson nods. "I knew you'd get it. Her train gets into Rensselaer around three. Henderson will give you our sign to use, and she'll find you. You can take my car."

I have a beat-up old Honda that I've been driving since high school. I keep it running but don't otherwise put a lot of money into it. Half the year it's parked on a Brooklyn street and there's no guarantee for its safety. Or that it'll even be there every morning. The only reason I still hang onto it is to haul my stuff to gigs, but now that I play with D'von, we use his van most of the time.

Needless to say, whatever Grayson's driving is probably a lot nicer. And I'm guessing cleaner too.

"No sweat. I'll sweet talk her like there's no tomorrow. She'll be putty in my hands before we hit I-90."

"Aren't you confident today?" Grayson laughs.

I want to tell him about the possible development with my show but now is not the time. We've got so much work to do on *Showman* and no time to do it in. I hope whoever this ace-in-the-hole is, she's willing to bust her ass like the rest of us do.

I get to the Rensselaer Rail Station and park in the short-term parking with only moments to spare before her train pulls in. I run my fingers through my hair and re-do the rubber band that holds most of it back. Grabbing the sign that Grayson gave me, I stand there like an idiot, waiting for a total stranger.

I really should've gotten a name or something. I have no idea who to expect.

The last person on the face of the Earth I was expecting was *her*.

No. Freakin. Way.

I pull my lips tightly together, mostly to keep the string of expletives from rushing out.

There I am, standing in the middle of a train station, holding a sign like a chump, only to find out I'm waiting to chauffeur Leslie Ann Moose back to The Edison. If it wouldn't totally screw over everyone at the theater, I'd hightail it out of here before she sees—

"JOSH!" Her voice echoes throughout the terminal, and her bags hit the ground with a thud. She's sprinting toward me and before I know it, her body is slamming into mine, her arms wrapping around my neck. I stagger back with the force, my own hands involuntarily encircling her waist to prevent us both from going ass over teakettle.

Her scent fills my nostrils, and immediately I'm sixteen again and so deeply in love I don't know what to do with myself.

No.

I will not go back there.

I cannot go back there.

It's a bad place. A dark place. A place that I will no longer frequent.

I push her away, trying not to be too forceful. "Leslie."

She stares at me, blinking those beautiful brown eyes.

"I guess I'm your ride back to The Edison." There's still hope in her face. Shit. I remember what I'm here to do. *Coax. Schmooze. Convince.* "It's good to see you again. Now let's get your bag and get on the road." I take a few steps toward her duffle bag. It's sizable and heavy, which makes me think she's planning on being here for a bit.

Even still, I can't blow this for Grayson.

Leslie doesn't say anything until we're back in Grayson's car. "Josh, I … I owe you an explanation."

She does. She totally does.

"It's fine. What's past is past. No need to dwell on it." Not like I've been thinking about it for the past decade or anything. I grip the steering wheel and try not to grind my molars down to dust before we get back to Hicklam. "In fact, let's not bring it up. We're starting over right now."

"But …"

"So, you're considering the role of Anne? It's a great role. I hope you're familiar with it. I think Grayson said he was going to send you the book. He said you had the music too. Maybe you want to review it. It's about forty-five minutes to the theater from here." I ramble on like a jerk. Anything to keep her from talking.

"Um, okay. Yeah, I've got the song."

"Why don't you look through it? Maybe start humming it out."

"I'm good. I can wait until we get there."

I glance over to see her flicking at the side of her fingernail.

"Well, the rest of the cast has already been in rehearsals for three days. Not to mention you've got to learn the aerial stuff. Have you ever been on the silks or lyra before?" It's not like I really even know what those are. They're phrases I've heard Jasmine and Levi bat about. I wouldn't know a silk if it hit me in the lyra.

The silence fills the car, thick and heavy. I probably shouldn't have said that. The Leslie I used to know was a perfectionist, striving to be the best in absolutely everything she did. Pointing out that everyone else already has a leg up on her probably wasn't the smartest thing.

But I've never been smart when it comes to Leslie. Obviously.

"I mean, I'm sure Grayson and Henderson and Kori have a plan to make it work for you. They obviously thought you were right for the part, otherwise, they wouldn't have called."

"No, they're desperate, and I fit the demographic they need. How many other black or brown actors do they have floating around?"

This is a chip she rightfully carries on her shoulder. "Actually, I think you'll find The Edison is pretty diverse." I run through a mental tally. "We have a standard company of eight male and eight female ensembles for every show. At least half of the company are actors of a minority. That doesn't include our leads."

She crosses her arms over her chest. "So then why do they want me?"

"Didn't you audition? Aren't you doing a show with us later this summer?"

"Well, yeah."

"Then they must have liked what they saw. The truth is Jasmine injured herself last night, so she can't do the part. There wasn't a long discussion before they contacted you. You must have stood out in their minds."

I have no idea what the conversation was behind closed office doors, but she doesn't need to know that. She just needs to feel that we want her.

Feeling wanted is more important than feeling needed.

Leslie doesn't say anything for a minute or two, and then I hear her humming softly. She's studying the music on her phone.

Good.

This way, I don't have to talk to her anymore.

My phone, connected to Grayson's car for the GPS, begins to ring. Mei's name pops up on the display. This should be interesting.

"Hey, babe. What's up?"

"Um, any chance you can come home this weekend? I got an offer for a gig out in the Hamptons. They'll put us up for the entire weekend, in addition to paying us our usual rates for Friday and Saturday nights."

Oh man, that would be a welcome influx of cash right about now.

"Mei, you know I can't. We open *Kiss Me, Kate* on Friday."

I can practically hear her indifferent shrug through the phone. We may share music, but her love is jazz, while mine is musical theater. She's hoping for a recording contract; I'm hoping for a show on Broadway. So close, yet so far away.

"Ugh. It's just that I haven't seen you in months."

I want to remind Mei that I've asked her several times to come up and see me, but she's always found a reason not to. On the other hand, I don't want to get into that in front of Leslie.

"I know. I miss you too." Okay, that might have been for Leslie's benefit. Truth be told, Mei hasn't even been on my mind that much. I'm sure that's a point that should be examined, but I've neither the time nor the energy to unpack that right now.

And definitely not in front of Leslie.

"But I think you should take the gig. See if Mark and D'von can go. I'm sure one of them knows another piano player."

"It is really good money. Plus, they're putting us up in fancy digs. I could use a little vacation out of the city."

I look at the countryside whirring by. It's definitely outside the city. "I know what you mean. But have a good time this weekend and let me know when you're coming up."

After I disconnect the call, I say the stupidest, most obvious thing ever. "That was my girlfriend."

I've never called Mei my girlfriend before. Mostly because she isn't. We're in some sort of loose, undefined physical relationship. We're not sleeping with anyone else, but it's not like there's this huge emotional piece for us.

Let's face it, I've done the all-in emotional piece before, and it did not work out well. I glance at Leslie again, who appears to be absorbed with her phone.

All that for her benefit, and she probably didn't even notice.

Good God, it's like I'm that desperate sixteen-year-old dork again.

That desperate sixteen-year-old dork who had his heart ripped out and decimated by the woman in the passenger's seat.

And just like that, I've never been in a worse mood.

Chapter 5: Leslie

That could've gone better. A lot better. Especially the part where I almost tackled him in the train station.

I forgot myself.

The minute I saw him, every single ounce of emotion came rushing back. It's a wonder I didn't flatten him right to the floor.

He said he's fine, but he's not. He's clenching his jaw so tight it's making mine hurt. His words are forced and guarded. And he definitely doesn't want to talk.

At least not to me. He seems to talk just fine to his girlfriend. Of course, he has a girlfriend. It's not like he'd wait all this time for me. Especially not after I ghosted him. He'd need his head examined if he was still interested in me.

I need my head examined.

I try to glance slyly at him out of the corner of my eye. I'm on the fence about his long hair. It's a different look for him, for sure. There's something else that's different about him too, but I can't put my finger on it. I mean, it's Josh. He looks like Josh. But there's something that's not familiar at all. Maybe it's just the passage of time. I'm sure I've changed a lot since I was sixteen.

At least I hope I have.

I didn't like myself much at sixteen. That was a big part of the reason I ended up at Stagehands Theatre Productions summer intensive camp. My parents, encouraged by my doctor, thought that keeping busy and rounding out my skills would fix all my problems. That if I took a summer off from ballet, I'd be cured.

News flash: I was not cured.

Oh sure, I put some weight back on and stopped obsessing. That is, I didn't obsess about ballet quite as much. Mostly because by the end, I was thinking about Josh.

Josh was the first person I talked to at STP, outside of my roommate, Chrissy McMillan. Chrissy could be easily typecast as "mean girl number one" and would nail it every time. Mostly because she was a mean girl armed with a brilliant smile, adorable good looks, a killer singing voice, and venom in her words.

After her first batch of scathing, backhanded compliments and thinly veiled insults, I went to find the phone to call my parents. There was no way I was going to be stuck in that hellhole for eight weeks, sharing a room with Satan.

"What group are you in?" the voice behind me asked.

I turned, not sure of what he was talking about. "Say what?"

"Are you an actor or a musician? They're two very separate worlds here, and never the two shall meet. Like North and South Korea."

"Well, that's a terrible comparison. People die in North Korea. Or is it South Korea?" I was rambling like an idiot. "The Korea with the mean government. Nobody should be dying here. If they are, we're in the plot of an entirely different movie than I signed up for. I don't want to be in a place where I need the odds to be ever in my favor."

He shrugged. "You know what I mean. So are you an actor or a musician?"

It was my turn to shrug. "I'm neither. I don't belong here, and I want to go home."

He folded his arms across his chest and nodded his head knowingly. "Oh. Mean roommate, right?"

I folded my arms to match his. "No," I scoffed. "Like I would let some mean girl with perfect hair and creamy skin scare me off in the first fifteen minutes. It's like you said—here you have to be an actor or a musician. I'm neither. I'm a dancer. A ballerina, to be exact. I shouldn't be here."

"Then why are you here?" He dropped his arms and leaned on the desk.

"My parents … thought I should be more well-rounded. They thought working on my acting would help with the robustness of my dance performance." It's not like I was going to admit why I was actually there.

"Robustness?" He raised his eyebrows.

"Yeah, I don't know what that means either."

A sly grin spread across his face. "Well, Robust, it was nice knowing you. It turns out, you are an actor, and I'm a musician, and so we are sworn mortal enemies." With that, he did a deep bend, like something out of an old movie. And I should know because my mom was obsessed with old movies.

"You've got quite the flair for the dramatic yourself there ... " I paused, not knowing his name.

"Josh. Josh deChambeau. Piano, guitar, and trumpet."

"Leslie. Leslie Ann Moose. Sidelined ballerina."

Josh nodded. "Leslie Ann Moose, I think you are a rule breaker."

I was not a rule breaker.

"Maybe." I shrugged.

"I think we should break the rules and be friends. What do you think?" He smiled and waggled his eyebrows at me.

That was a rule I was willing to break.

"You know, I was never a rule breaker. At least not until I met you." The words tumble out of my mouth, my brain forgetting that Josh wasn't there for my mental trip down memory lane.

"What?" He turns to look at me, the car swerving with his movement.

"Watch it! I mean, when we first met, you said I looked like a rule breaker. I wasn't. I never had been. I'm still not. The only time I broke the rules was with you."

"Uh-huh. I highly doubt that."

"No, it's true. I follow the rules. I work hard. It's the only way to be the best. If you cheat, then even if you win, you didn't earn it."

He gives me another side glance. "How's that working out for you?"

Like shit.

"Well, I'm here. I've worked hard and paid my dues, and someone finally realized it. And I'll work hard with this, and maybe they'll see that I deserve a better role. Or an actual role. Not just the understudy."

"So you've finally made the jump from dance to theater? See—I knew you were an actor. You can definitely put on the performance when you need to."

Wait—was that an insult?

He continues, "I can't believe it's taken you ten years to come to the conclusion I made in ten seconds." His words seem playful and nostalgic. However, there's an underlying bite to his tone that doesn't sit well with me.

I get it. I hurt him. I'll just have to show him that I'm not that same girl who didn't know how to balance everything.

I mean, I'm still not sure I've figured it out. I have more time for dating, but only because I failed at being a ballerina. I'm not really sure that's the balance most life coaches talk about. Maybe I could meme it. *Find your balance: fail at your dream so you have time for other stuff.*

I could totally see that on a pillow. Or a mug.

Maybe I should get into the merch business to pay my bills. If this doesn't work out, I should buy one of those Cricut things.

We pull into a winding driveway that leads up a hill. I swear The Edison's compound looks like something out of a movie set. The theater itself is a large building with a sweeping circular driveway out in front. Large posters set up on wooden legs, advertising the upcoming shows greet us, like flags outside the United Nations. There is a courtyard, and gardens and arbors covered in greens and flowers. Quaint is the word for it. Behind the theater are more nondescript buildings that look like post-WWII dorms. They're the least attractive thing here. Off to the side is the most charming farmhouse, complete with a white, painted porch and hanging flower baskets. There are parking lots and walking trails, and what looks like a barn or woodshop. It's got a great view of the town below.

It's freakin' adorable.

"This place would make a great camp."

"We have one here. It's a day camp. I think it starts in two weeks. The kids come every day for three weeks and then do a production at the end. *Newsies* this year. Gloria runs it."

"That's great. You guys really have it all here." I step out of the car.

"Let me show you where the dorms are so you can drop your stuff."

I head to the rear of the car to get my bags when it hits me how presumptuous he's being. "I haven't committed yet. I could be back on a train tonight."

Josh looks at my stuffed backpack and oversized duffle also filled to the gills. "You brought a lot of stuff for an afternoon."

I raise my eyebrow at him, trying to look mysterious. In reality, I'm pissed that he saw right through me.

"Come on, Leslie. This is big. We're doing a pre-workshop for *The Greatest Showman*. If it goes well, they're likely going to workshop it for Broadway. It'll be huge, not only for The Edison but for the cast. It's a make-or-break show for us. Don't dick us around. Don't dick *me* around. Again." And then he turns and walks away, leaving me standing there at the car.

Shit.

If I don't accept this, I'll be letting everyone here down. I'll be letting Josh down. I've already done that enough for one lifetime. I haul my bags out of the car and slam the trunk shut. Unsure of where to go next, I head into the theater.

The first person I see is Henderson, the guy from auditions. "Oh, number seventy-two. You're here. Welcome. Are you ready to get started?"

He's all business. Okay, that's the tone. I can certainly match it.

"Where can I put my stuff? Do I need to change?" I look down at my ripped jeans and tank top.

"Prolly. Dressing rooms are back that way." He nods toward the stage. "You can use a room there. You can chuck your bags there for the moment. Jasmine is banged up and groggy, but she might be able to get you started. If not, Levi can help. At least show you some basics and figure out what you can do. And you remember Kori from auditions? She'll be working with you on choreography. We figure we'll supplement the aerial tricks that Jasmine was going to do with some of your dance skills."

I think this is the most I've ever heard Henderson say at one time.

Five minutes later, I'm standing in the barn—the only rehearsal space other than the actual stage with a ceiling high enough for this—clad in leggings and my tank top, feet bare, and thinking that I might want to puke. It's not that I'm afraid of heights. It's more that I'm afraid of falling.

There's definitely the potential to fall.

The metaphorical falling.

"We're going to have to perform without a mat, so once you learn it, we're taking the mats away," Kori announces. She's not even waiting to rip the Band-Aid off.

"Don't worry, honey. It seems a lot worse than it is," Levi adds. He's playing the role of Philip in the show, and I'll have most of my scenes with him. "You don't even really have to do anything. I mean you don't have to fly if you don't want to."

"If you can get a little off the ground, that'd be great. Ready to try?" The bandaged hand indicates this is Jasmine. "We're just using a silk hammock and the lyra hoop for this show. Have you ever used either?"

I shake my head.

She points to the large loop of fabric hanging down from a rope and carabiner. It's about three feet or so off the ground.

"Let's warm you up. You're going to be sore as it is, so we should minimize that," Kori says. "Levi, can you show her your stretching routine?"

Levi begins walking me through a bunch of yoga stretches that I'm quite familiar with. It feels good to be limbering up. Because of my muscle bulk, I'm not the most flexible dancer in the world, but compared to the average person, I'm pretty stretchy. My joints pop and crack, and I resist the urge to groan into some of the deeper stretches.

Let's face it, compared to the average person, I'm not bulky either, but the world of ballet is far from average.

"You look good. You're going to have beautiful lines, I can tell," Jasmine says. I look over to her, and I swear she's crying. I glance at Levi, who just shakes his head.

"Stay focused," he whispers. "We have a lot to do."

I'm used to dancing for several hours at a clip with only small breaks. But after ninety minutes with the silk hammock, I want to die. Mostly, my arms want to die. I'm not sure I'll ever be able to lift them again. I should have taken Josh up on his offer to carry my bags to my room because there's no way I'm hauling those puppies now.

On the other hand, I can go upside down and do a few other tricks with some relative grace. I didn't fall and break my neck. I did, however, manage to give myself the mother of all wedgies with the large swath of fabric as I attempted to slide down into a split. I think my clothing is now inside my body. This could impact my ability to have kids someday. *Ouch*. Still, it's a lot harder than I'd expected, but I'm doing it. I'm sure it's nothing compared to what Jasmine could do, but I don't feel terrible about myself.

That's a start for me.

Chapter 6: Josh

S he looks good.

I thought she was beautiful when we were teens but being an adult suits her better. Her posture is impeccable, but I'd expect nothing less from someone who gave up everything else in life for ballet.

Why is she here?

She never wanted to be an actor. Only ever a dancer. A ballerina. A principal ballerina, to be exact.

What happened?

I don't know tons about dance, but she seems good. Or at least she was. Maybe she's injured in some way. But if that were the case, would she take a role she knew would be physically demanding? Not to mention, she's the understudy for the lead in *An American in Paris*.

I shake my head and rake my fingers through my hair. No, I shouldn't be thinking about her like this.

I hate her.

I want to hate her.

I should hate her.

What kind of person just disappears? Ten years ago, the term "ghosting" didn't exist, but that's exactly what she did.

Once we left STP, it was like I never existed for her. Or she no longer existed for me. Except she did. She took up a lot more mental space than I care to admit. Maybe I didn't actually need her, but I thought I did because of my parents.

It was a lot to lose all at once.

But I thought we were friends—more even—and when I needed her most, she wasn't there for me. Hell, she *blocked* me.

Grayson slides up to me. "How was the ride? Does she seem interested?"

I think about the way she practically tackled me. "Yes, I think she'll stay."

"Good. She's in with Kori, Levi, and Jas now, so we'll see what they have to say. She's got a lot of ground to make up."

"She's a hard worker."

Grayson cocks his head. "How do you know?"

Damn. I wasn't going to tell anyone. Mostly because I don't want them seeing what a fool she made of me.

"I mean, she's a professional ballerina, isn't she? Isn't that what you said? You don't get there by coasting."

"True. I'm not sure what her voice is like. H, man, come here," Grayson yells to Henderson, who is speed walking by. Henderson's always in a rush or grumpy. Those are pretty much his two moods.

"S'up, mate?"

"How was Leslie's voice at the audition? Josh here wants to know what he's in for."

Henderson gazes toward the ceiling trying to recall. "Um, I reckon quite decent. If it weren't for the name bit, I prolly would've cast her as Lise."

"Name bit?"

"Yeah, mate. She didn't put a name on her application. She said she was torn about using a stage name. She should totally use a stage name." Henderson shrugs. "But you know me. I don't like drama, and that one had drama written all over her."

Can't say he's wrong there.

Grayson narrows his eyes a bit. "I still don't buy it."

Henderson shrugs. "Well, maybe it was because you were up my arse about having Tabitha come out here. Also more drama."

Grayson playfully punches Henderson on the arm. "Ah, now we get down to the truth."

A stage name.

It would make sense. She's always been sensitive about it. It's an unfortunate name, especially for someone in her profession. But on the other hand, that's a crappy reason to lose out on a role.

But that's the thing with auditions—you never know the one thing you'll say or do that will end up either sealing the deal or breaking it for you. This business is not for the weak-spirited, that's for sure.

My dad always said that. *You've got to have a strong will and thicker skin. Let it all roll off you.*

"What'd she sing?" Grayson asks.

Henderson's staring up at the ceiling again as if it holds all the secret answers. I glance up too, just to make sure it doesn't. "Um, I think *Les Mis*," he replies.

And with those two words, the memories I've been desperate to keep locked away come rushing back.

"I have to sing." She flopped down on my bed, hands covering her face.

"Duh." I pulled out a Twizzler from the pack and then tossed the rest to Leslie. "Have some sugar. It'll make things better."

She uncovered her face and glanced over at the candy. "No, thanks." Her hands covered her face again. "What am I going to do? I can't sing."

"Maybe not yet, but you can learn."

"No, I can't. Singing isn't something you learn. It's a talent you're either born with or not."

I loved this debate, mostly because I loved proving people wrong. "So you're saying I could never learn a dance step because I'm not inherently talented at dancing?"

"Of course not. You can learn a certain level of proficiency. You may not be ready for the Bolshoi, but you could look decent."

I held my hand out to her, and hesitantly, she took it. I pulled her to her feet.

"Stick with me, kid, and I'll have you belting out Les Mis *before the end of camp. You'll want to use it every time you audition."*

She's still using that piece.

It was perfect for her, that alto range.

Shit. Alto range.

"Henderson, we may have an issue. What is she?" I have to ask to cover my tracks, even though I know what he's going to say.

"Alto, I think."

I begin flipping through the score until I find her song. With my finger tracing the notes, I find what I feared. "The top note she has to hit is an E♭5. If Leslie's an alto, that typically only goes to D5. It's only a half-step higher, but still. Do you know if she can hit that note? Especially while she's in midair? Do you really think she can do this? If she can't, we need to know now."

"So you need to get her in the music room."

"As soon as possible."

I glance down at my watch. "We're going to have to start *Kate* soon. I'm not going to have time to teach her this. She's going to have to be a natural."

She is not a natural, not unless she's been in vocal lessons for the past ten years. It took me eight weeks to get her proficient ten years ago. We don't have eight weeks.

It's probably too early to declare that this is hopeless, but that fear is there, and it's real. Especially knowing Leslie's track record when the going gets tough.

She gets gone.

"You wanna see how they're doing in there?" Maybe she'll be an epic failure on the silks, and I won't have to worry about her being here for the next five weeks.

Seeing her every day for the next five weeks.

It took me less than that to fall in love with her the first time. Hell, it only took five minutes. Okay, maybe ten. How could I not fall in love? Beautiful brown skin, sexy curls, taut muscles, a plump ass, and boobs to match? I mean, I was also a horny teenager, so none of that was a stretch. In reality, it was her drive. Her determination. How her eyes would light up when she'd talk about becoming the first brown principal ballerina.

I knew that hunger. I felt it too. I still do. I look at my score and book, now spanning several notebooks, and understand her desire. When you want something so bad you can taste it. That it consumes you day and night, until there's very little left of you, and only that want in its place.

I can't even tally up the number of social events and time with friends I've given up to work on my show. But every time I work on it, I don't regret it. All artists have to sacrifice for their craft. If they didn't, everyone would do it.

"Why don't you check? I need to grab a quick bite before we start the next round." I'm only vaguely aware that I'm even hungry, but I don't want to spend any more time with Leslie than I have to.

A few minutes later, Henderson returns. I'm still sitting at my piano. Normally when I'm doing this, I'm running through some kind of composition or another. Today is different. The only thing I'm running through is memories.

I looked down, her sepia legs entwined with mine. This late in the summer, my tan skin was only a shade or two lighter than hers. I threaded my fingers through hers, mixing our flesh once more. "I can't believe we have to leave in a little while."

"My parents are probably pulling in now. My mom's a freak about punctuality. She says it's rude and disrespectful to be late."

I pushed myself into a sitting position, my legs stretched out in front of me. I hauled Leslie up so she was sitting against my chest. Again, I entwined my fingers in hers. "Are you going to introduce me to your parents?"

Her hands went still in mine. I closed my eyes, not wanting to hear the words I feared were coming. As the silence stretched between us, my stomach dropped further and further. "This is more than a summer fling. You know that."

She turned herself around to face me, straddling my lap. She took my face in her hands. "This was more than a fling. But you'll be in New Hampshire, and I'll be in Ohio."

"Yes, but those are just places. What we have—what we feel—it's more than just places. We can make it work. And we only have two years until college. Then we can be together. Until then, we can find a way."

It never occurred to me that she didn't want to find a way. That she had no intention of planning our schooling together. That she had no intention of even keeping in touch. In that moment, I felt so deeply.

I've never felt that way again.

And because of Leslie Ann Moose, I probably never will again.

Chapter 7: Leslie

Okay, that's probably enough for today, and we've got to run through *Kiss Me, Kate,*" Kori says. "You need to learn the song so that we can start marking this tomorrow. Do you have the music?"

I nod. "I have it on my phone, but the sheet music would be helpful. Is there someone who can work on it with me?"

Of course, I mean Josh, but I can't come right out and say that. He taught me to sing once before. I know he can do it again.

Plus, I want to see him again.

It's not like I was really over him when I moved on. I simply didn't have enough spoons in my mental drawer to have him in my life. Not with everything else I was dealing with.

Unfortunately, you can't ghost your inferiority complex or eating disorder.

Kori looks at Levi. "Um, who's not in *Kate*?"

He shrugs in return. "Tabitha, but she's usually with Henderson. Maybe Gloria would help you?"

This must be the same Gloria Josh mentioned; the one who runs the camp. "Where can I find her to ask?"

"Come with me." Levi grabs my hand and tugs gently. Just the act of moving my arm away from my body is starting to be painful. It's going to be a long week while my body acclimates to this new form of exertion. "So, tell me about yourself, my beautiful African queen."

"Well, I'm not African, but in my head, I've always deserved to be treated like royalty, so you may keep that."

Levi stops. "Oh, I'm sorry, honey. Are you Dominican? Mexican? I want to be culturally sensitive." He guides me through the door and we head toward some of the other rooms. I think this is where they work on costumes and sets.

"Fijian." And then I wait.

Ah, there it is. The furrowed brow, the look of confusion. "Like Mount Fiji?"

"That's Fuji."

"Oh, like the water." He grins, nodding his head sagely.

This is not the first time I've had this conversation.

"Yes, just like that." Truth be told, I have no idea if the water actually comes from Fiji anymore. I still buy it because I like to think I'm supporting my grandparents' country. Sadly, I've only been there twice, and not since I was about thirteen.

Another sacrifice I made for ballet.

If I ever made a list of all the things I gave up for ballet versus all the positive things it gave me, I'm afraid it would be very lopsided.

Without waiting for Levi to ask because everyone always does, I explain, "Fiji is considered Polynesia and is called the 'crossroads of the Pacific.' It's about thirteen hundred miles off the coast of New Zealand. You ever heard of the golfer Vijay Singh? He's Fijian. We also have the worlds' best rugby, hands down."

"If you say so. Golf is so boring." Levi rolls his eyes. "And rugby is so ..." he wrinkles his nose and flips his hand, "burly and dirty."

"Yes, but those rugby players are tough, and they all have very nice-looking thighs. That's why I watch it." It's not—even though I'm only half-Fijian, being a die-hard rugby fan is in my blood. Most Americans don't understand that.

However, most people do understand a shapely thigh.

Levi is one of those people. "Girl, maybe you piqued my interest." He drops my hand, instead looping his arm through mine. *Ouch*.

This soreness in my arms does not bode well. My legs and feet are used to taking the brunt of my work.

"I'll let you know the next time a match is on."

"Here she is. Gloria, darling." He leans in to air kiss the cheeks of the woman who paused in the middle of sorting costumes to smile at us. "Are you available to help Leslie with some music? She's come in for Jasmine."

She nods. "Let's go into the rehearsal room." I follow her as she walks away. Gloria is one of those petite brunette beauties that I've always envied. I glance down. Yep. Small feet.

It's not that my feet are that large. They're just wide and flat. Not ballet feet. Finding pointe shoes was always tough because, in addition to ballerinas being pale, they're supposed to have slender feet as well.

I should have known then I wasn't going to make it.

"So, they called you in to save the day? They did that to me last season. No pressure or anything."

I smile. "I guess. It sounds like this show is super important."

Gloria pulls open a door and flips on the light in a large room. There are tables and chairs stacked up in a corner and music stands littering the floor. An upright piano stands front and center, commanding an audience.

"With the way finances run in a theater like this, every show is important. But this one more so. One, because of the workshop potential, but two, because of Tabitha Stetson."

The name sounds vaguely familiar, but I can't quite place why.

Gloria sees the confusion on my face. "Tabby Cat from the Sassy Cats. She's in this show."

Shut the front door.

And, oh crap.

This just ratcheted up the pressure. Like I need any more of that.

I kind of want to puke.

We make our way to the piano. "I'm not much of a piano player, so we'll see what we can do."

"That's good because I'm not much of a singer. We're probably well-matched." I smile at her. "And I can't play the piano to save my life, so you're automatically better than me. I would like to do a vocal warm-up before I try. It's been a while since I've had to sing." The audition was in March, which was three months ago. These pipes are bound to be rusty.

Gloria is patient and doesn't laugh at me too much. Her voice is incredible. I'll never sound like her. I could work day and night and I won't be that good. But I have to be good enough. This whole show is depending on me.

I can't believe I'm in the "good enough" mindset.

After what feels like forever, Gloria suggests a break. "I need to get some water." She stands up from the piano and glances around. "Do you have any?"

I shake my head. "Nah, I got started as soon as I arrived. Hell, my bags are still in one of the dressing rooms." I think. I hope.

"Have you eaten at all?"

I'm about to say I'm not hungry, but my stomach growls in betrayal. You'd think I'd be used to my stomach betraying my brain after all these years.

"Okay, let's head up to the kitchen. The kitchen's stocked and there are prepared meals in the fridge. You can certainly get your own food too. Just label it. And clean up after yourself. There's no maid, and the quickest way to become enemy number one is to leave your dirty dishes out."

"I'm used to roommates, so I get that. Do I contribute for the food? How does this all work?"

"The basics and staples are part of the deal. It's why the salary isn't spectacular. The room and board are factored in with that. But the food is basic. Linda either cooks for the midday meal, which is usually the big one, or has food brought in. There are always fruits and veggies, cereals, breads, granola bars, yogurt, sandwich fixin's, and that kind of stuff. If you want something more, rock on with your big bad self. People are always doing Wal-Mart runs in their downtime. But that's mostly for booze and energy drinks."

I can't see myself buying any extra food, but if they don't have the right choices for me, I might have to. Even after all this time, it's still an occasional battle.

We walk over to the dorms and my legs are threatening to go on strike. And they're the better functioning of my limbs. I hope every door I have to open is a push because I don't think I can pull anything.

This is going to suck.

I'm sure I'm going to have to go back and do some more tonight. I mean, I totally have to. I'm so lost and behind, I might never catch up.

I will not be the one who brings this show down.

Even though I try to deny being hungry, once Gloria brings me into the kitchen, suddenly I'm ravenous. I pour a large glass of water and drink that first before I even look at anything else.

"What are you in the mood for?" Gloria asks, opening the fridge and peering at the contents.

My famished stomach speaks for me. "My dad's curry."

Gloria turns, tilting her head. "I didn't have you pegged for Indian."

I smile. "I'm not. My dad's family is from Fiji. Curry is their go-to dish."

"My lola—grandmother—is from the Philippines, and she used to make a killer fish curry. I miss it. Can't get that here in Hicklam, that's for sure."

I know what she means. It's hard to find traditional Fijian foods anywhere, so we only had it on those rare occasions my dad cooked. "My mom's family is from Ohio, so bratwurst is her default. Makes for interesting potluck family events."

Gloria perks up. "Ohio? I'm from Ohio. Where?"

"Delaware County. Where are you from?"

"Other side of Columbus. Licking County. Granville."

We stand there for a minute, and then a wide grin spreads across my face. "What are the odds that we'd both end up acting here in Hicklam?"

Gloria laughs. "If you only knew. I didn't end up here for The Edison. In fact, it was the furthest thing from my mind."

"With a voice like yours? I'm surprised Broadway isn't beating a path to your door."

Her gaze drops to the floor as she inhales deeply. "I actually moved to Hicklam to work with a therapist who specializes in the treatment of PTSD. I ... I was the victim of revenge porn." She stops and shudders. "I hate that term, but that's what it was. It left me paralyzed with fear and anxiety for nearly ten years.

I never pictured myself getting back on stage—I could barely leave the house. But I met Grayson and ended up working on the renovations here."

There's a lot here to unpack. "Like the *actual* renovations?"

"Like full-on HGTV drywall and painting and tiling renovations. Tool belts and power tools and the whole nine yards. Being around the theater was a trigger for me, but the therapy worked. I even got back on stage, mostly because they were screwed."

"Now that's true love right there."

She laughs. "It is, but not the kind you're thinking of. While I love Grayson—I'm even gonna marry him someday—I didn't do it for him. I did it for me. I had to take back the power that they stole from me. Getting my power back was a big piece of my healing."

I stand there for a minute. "I'm not sure whether to say that's terrible or awesome."

"It's messed up, but I'm happy now."

"So are you two officially engaged? I thought they said you were Grayson's girlfriend?"

Gloria grins sheepishly. "Technically, he asked and I said yes, but I'm not ready yet. I can't marry him until I know I'm well enough. I'm still doing that work. I wish I was better already. I wish I could marry him right now. Well, not right now because the schedule's crazy. But there are so many things I wish. I wish I hadn't lost those years." She pauses, thinking. "Actually, I wish those assholes hadn't violated my trust and my body in the first place, but you can't control what others do. You can only control yourself and your reaction."

I can relate deeply to what Gloria means. I've never been happy enough or satisfied enough with myself to be able to be happy with another person. I mean, if I don't like me, why should anyone else? And if they do, there's probably something wrong with them, and they're not worth dating.

"Well, if The Edison doesn't work out for you, you could always make a career out of creating inspirational memes. That's my backup plan. I've already got my eye on a Cricut."

Gloria laughs. "It's good to have a backup plan. Now, what do you want to eat?"

My stomach pangs with hunger. "I'll just make myself a salad."

Maybe I should consider asking Gloria for her therapist's number.

KATHRYN R. BIEL

Chapter 8: Josh

I like being in rehearsal for *Kiss Me, Kate.* Not only is Cole Porter's music fun to play, but it means Leslie isn't here.

Not that she's not occupying space in my brain.

Space I did not give her permission to occupy.

But even as Amy sings "So in Love," I find myself wondering how Leslie's making out. Is she going to stay? Of course, she is. Can she do the role? That remains to be seen.

We need her to succeed. The Edison depends on it. The future of this show depends on it. Yet, I know somewhere deep down I don't want her to succeed. If she's the person she showed me ten years ago, the thing she values the most in the world—above everything and everyone else—is being a success. Being the best.

It's petty, I know, but I don't want her to have that. Someone who can be so careless and cruel doesn't deserve to get everything they want in life.

Okay, that's harsh and immature. She can be successful, but I don't have to be happy about it.

I shoot Mei a text. I'm not even sure why I do. Maybe I don't want her to think I'm not thinking about her. Maybe I want her to know that even though I'm here and she's there, I'm not ghosting her. It's not like she's the love of my life or anything, but I'm trying to be a nice guy here.

Or I'm trying to make up for the vengeful thoughts that have been flooding my mind about Leslie all day.

Seriously, out of all the theaters in the world, she's got to walk into mine?

It's fine. I'll just have as little to do with her as possible, and before I know it, the time will be up, and she'll disappear for another decade. I hope.

Finally, we're done and closing up for the night. I see a light on in the dance room. No matter how Grayson and Henderson go on and on about saving electricity, someone always leaves something on somewhere.

As I push open the door, I realize it's not just a light carelessly left burning. It's Leslie, practicing on the silks. Her back is to me, and I watch as she grasps the material, putting her foot in. She extends that leg gracefully in front of her, her toes pointed in the hammock. With a contraction of her arms, she hoists herself up to standing, her back arching gracefully as her free leg floats up in front of her. This leg then swings out to the side and suddenly she's doing some sort of split, suspended in midair. She lets go with one hand, arching back, dangling like she's done this for years. She moves her leg up and around the fabric, twisting, and then all of a sudden, she's hanging upside down, her arms gracefully posing, as years of ballet have trained her to do.

At which point, she sees me. I know this because of the blood-curdling scream she lets out as her legs begin to flail and she gets more twisted. The silks begin to spin the more she squirms to get out.

Rushing forward, it's not until I reach her that I realize I have no idea how to begin extracting her from this tangle of red fabric.

"Stop it. Stop!"

I'm not sure if she's yelling at me or the apparatus. Maybe a little of both.

I grab the fabric, unsuccessful in avoiding her thrashing limbs. She strikes my legs and torso. Ouch.

"What are you doing?" she yells.

"Trying to help you out. Stop kicking me." I finally get to a point where I can stabilize the hammock. Leslie begins to try to reach up and haul herself upright. Her legs are all twisted up, spread apart like in some torture device. Her butt hangs below her levels, and unless she has abs of steel, I don't see any way she's going to get back upright to sitting in this thing.

"Oh God, I can't. My arms are spent. I don't think I can get myself out of this."

Letting go of the fabric, I grab her under her arms and try to pull her upright. At the height she's dangling, she's not too far off the ground, but also just high enough to make this awkward.

"Stop. I've got an idea." This time, she lets herself fall backward, reaching toward the ground. "Okay," she pants. "Can you untwist this leg?" She wiggles her foot, pushing her leg out.

I reach up and unloop the fabric. As her limb is finally freed, she slides down, catching her weight on her hands for a moment, before collapsing to the ground, her other leg held upright and entangled in the fabric. Quickly I work to free her. Her leg flops to the floor.

For a moment, she lies there on the ground, panting heavily. "You scared the crap out of me. I could have gotten hurt."

"Well, you shouldn't be in here by yourself. You could have gotten hurt and no one would know."

"You were all busy. And I've got a lot of catching up to do."

I look down at her, splayed across the floor. "You've been in here all this time?"

"Gloria and I worked on music and then we ate. I thought I'd try to practice what Levi and Jasmine showed me earlier."

I cock my eyebrow. "So you're going to stay then, I take it?"

She closes her eyes, a faint grin spreading across her face. "You knew it all along, so don't sound so surprised."

"Well, I'm heading to the dorms. You coming?"

"Do you even know where I'm staying? I don't."

I sigh. I see how this is going to go. "I'll show you. I think there's a bed somewhere. Let me text Grayson to see what room you're in."

While I'm on my phone, I see her get up from the floor slowly. She's definitely moving gingerly. Her arms are hanging down, but slightly away from her sides. I follow her to the dressing room where her bags have been shoved in a corner. Leslie stands there, staring at them.

"Okay, Grayson says there's an empty bed in Amy's room. You can stay there."

"Okay." Her voice is quiet. She's still just staring at her bags.

"Are you trying to move them with mental telepathy or something? Let's go. Tomorrow's the last day before *Kate* opens, so it's going to be a long one. I'd like to go to bed."

Shit. I shouldn't have said it like that. What if she thinks that's an invitation? There's no way in hell that's happening ... again. That was then, and this is now. She is dead to me as far as I'm concerned.

She turns to look at me, her dark eyes wide. "What?" I ask, not bothering to hide my impatience.

"Give me a minute. I'm trying to work up the strength to pick these up. I'm not sure I can."

I look at the bags, knowing how heavy they were. I also think about what I saw her doing on the silks. "How long were you in there for?"

Her shoulders lift up and then quickly sag. "Well, I did about an hour and a half earlier with Levi, Kori, and Jasmine, and ... what time is it now?"

"Twelve-thirty."

"So yeah, about three more hours."

"Jesus, Leslie, what were you thinking? You're going to die tomorrow."

"Nah, the day after that will be much worse. Do you know if there's a bathtub here? I'm probably going to need to soak a bit."

"Why did you do that? Practice so long?"

Leslie tilts her head. "Come on, I know it's been a while, but do I really have to tell you?"

"Yes, because I'm not sure I even know you."

"Josh, how can you say that? Of course you know me."

I raise my eyebrows. "Do I? You certainly weren't the person I thought you were. Now tell me, why would you push yourself like that?"

"I'm behind. I have to learn. I can't get out there and fail. Not again. So I'll put in the hard work if that's what it takes."

"Don't you think this is a little extreme? Three hours?"

"If it's what I need to do to get the job done, then no. If it's what The Edison needs to make this show a success, then no."

You gotta admire that work ethic. I bend over, picking up her bags. "I'll show you to your room."

Walking in silence, we finally make it to the dorms. Right before we turn to go in, Leslie says, "Are you still mad at me? It was so long ago."

Hell yes, I'm mad.

But it's more than that. I can't extract my feelings about her from the feelings about my parents and the accident. I needed her to help me work through them, and she wasn't there for me. So yes, I'm mad. And sad. And hurt. But I'm not telling her any of that. She doesn't have the right to know.

I just shrug. "Here you go. Amy, this is Leslie. Leslie, this is Amy. Rehearsal starts at eight."

I drop her bags just inside the door and turn around without saying anything else. I don't want to talk about the past. I don't want to talk about ourselves now. I don't want to be around her.

Because whether I want to admit it or not, I can see myself getting sucked back in. The desire's there. But it's taken me so long to move on from those complex feelings. I can't let her derail me on my journey. Not when I'm so close to getting what I want. But as I sit down on my bed and pull out my notebook, it hits me like a ton of bricks. I look over at my nightstand to see the well-worn copy of Oscar Wilde's *The Importance of Being Earnest*. I pick up the book, hurling it across the room.

I flip through the pages of my notebook, reading the lyrics I've written. Looking at the script I've roughed out. It's right there on the page, in black and white.

The careless deception.

Jesus Christ, my whole damn show is about Leslie.

WHATEVER IT TAKES

Chapter 9: Leslie

I think you're good to go in here for now. You've nailed enough of the basics to make this work. You can't really do much more until you know the music. You need to work with Josh now," Kori says, packing up her notebook. I look at Jasmine, cradling her bandaged hand. "Do you think so? Should I be working with the lyra a little more?"

After I'd figured out some tricks on the silk hammock, we moved onto the aerial hoop. It's supposed to be harder, but it's a lot more static poses. The metal of the hoop is hard, and the front of my legs and sides of my hips are covered with bruises. Jasmine assures me that'll go away, and that the calluses will firm up on my hands. Using copious amounts of chalk helps that. My hands have never looked this pale. They're almost my mom's color. My feet are normally calloused and gross from my pointe shoes, so this is not new to me. I think it'll be easier to sing on the lyra than on the silks, but we're still figuring it out.

Because in the past three days, I haven't worked on the song at all. At least not with Josh.

I've been avoiding him like the plague. And I think he's been avoiding me too.

He says he's not mad at me, but he totally is. He should be. I still am. It's another thing on my long list of failures. Someday, I'm going to need a separate trailer just to haul all my baggage around with me.

"Go find Josh." Kori points to the door. "You'd better catch up with him quickly. The matinee starts at one, so he's usually doing sound checks by noon or so, and it's already ten-thirty."

Jasmine smiles. "This is looking good. You're better than I hoped. Now you need your vocals to be strong. Make sure you focus on your diaphragm. When you're up in the air, all the power has to come from there, otherwise, you'll sound wobbly."

I wander into the music room. Josh is sitting at the piano, staring off into space.

"Hey," I say softly, not wanting to startle him. "Kori says I have to work on my vocals."

He nods and flips the pages of his binder. Without waiting for me to cross the room, he starts on the intro for "Rewrite the Stars."

"Wait, I need to warm up. Someone once told me that my voice is a precious instrument that needs tender care, and that I should never take it from zero to sixty without preparation."

"That person sounds like a pretentious ass."

With my lips pressed tightly together, I grin slightly. "It's still good advice. I wouldn't make you do a split without stretching you first."

"You'd never get me to do a split, not without removing my legs from my body first, so no worries there." He may be giving me a hard time, but he shifts into playing the chords for warmups. Wringing my hands, I take my place at the music stand opposite him. After about fifteen minutes of oohing and aahing and me-may-ma-mo-moo'ing, I'm ready to go.

I think.

"Okay, you're definitely still an alto. We're going to drop you down a register and start at Bb3. It should be more comfortable for you there." Josh pulls out a pencil and scribbles something on his music.

"Did Jasmine have to sing it there?"

He looks up. "Everyone sings where they need to be. If we were in the casting process, maybe we'd look for a mezzo rather than an alto. We're just going to make it work for you."

"Am I copping out? I can try it where it's supposed to be. I'll work on it. I'll make it happen."

Josh slams his hand down on the piano. "Jesus, Leslie. Not everything in life is something you have to bulldoze your way through. Sometimes just accept where you are. Which is an alto."

Maybe it's exhaustion. Maybe it's because every muscle in my body is screaming with pain and fatigue. Maybe it's because I'm terrified that I won't be able to do this. It doesn't matter why, but my eyes fill up.

Josh purses his lips together, forming a tight, straight line. "I didn't mean to make you cry."

"I'm not crying."

"Then why are your eyes all wet?"

"I'm not crying. I don't cry."

He tilts his head ever so slightly. Even though I know him, he seems so different to me. He was my first love. My first kiss. My first ... everything. And now he's sitting here, and he doesn't even look like the Josh I carried in my heart all these years.

Cue the waterworks.

"Um, Leslie, for someone who doesn't cry, your eyes are really leaking."

"No, they're not." Angrily, I wipe the tears away. "You need to get your eyes examined. There must be something wrong with them." I take a deep breath. "Okay, I'm ready."

Josh starts on the music again. Right before it's my cue to come in, he says, "You know, this is the register Zendaya sang in. You're not taking the easy way out. You're playing your instrument how it should be played." And then he lifts his eyebrows to let me know my cue.

After a while of putting me through the paces, Josh stops playing and says, "I'm going to have to get something to eat before the craziness starts. Why don't you record this on your phone so you can practice this afternoon? I think you need to spend some time on your vocals."

That's his polite way of saying that I suck.

I drop my head, trying to absorb the blow.

"Leslie, you're not doing bad, but we both know that this is your weakest area. You'll be fine—you've definitely got the potential to do this well. You just need to put in the heavy lifting." He stands up from the piano and closes the distance between us. Gingerly, he puts a finger under my chin and tilts my head up. "You can absolutely do this. I know you're not afraid of the work. You're never afraid of the work. You may be afraid of a lot of things, but work isn't one of them."

Immediately, my mind flashes to right after camp, when I blocked Josh from all my social media. Hell, I wasn't even back in Ohio when I blocked him. I had no idea how to split my focus. How to even approach a balance, so I cut him out. I was definitely afraid of that work.

"That's not always true."

He must sense what I'm talking about. His hand falls, leaving a cold, empty space where his touch had been.

He sits down and nods at me to get my phone out. I do, and we record a few takes, including some piano for me to try to match notes with.

"Okay, that should help. Now let's go get some lunch. I hear Linda made lasagna today."

I take a deep breath, telling my inner critic that fuel for my engine is a good thing. "Sounds good," I say tightly.

We walk in silence to the kitchen in the dorms. There's a large dining room with long tables and benches stretching the length. It's pretty full. It seems the entire cast and crew is pre-game fueling. As they should be.

Food is lined up on the kitchen counter. Josh and I grab plates and begin dishing up. I stack my plate with fruits and veggies, but I can't resist a small piece of lasagna. I follow Josh into the dining room, thinking about how we ate all our meals together at STP.

Except now, he's wedged himself in between two members of the pit band. I scan the room, feeling just like I did in high school.

Never fitting in.

Amy waves. "Come on over. We can make room." She is seriously the nicest person I've ever met, and not at all like the shrew character she plays in *Kiss Me, Kate.* "Leslie, you know everyone, right?"

I've at least seen most of their faces, though I'm still trying to attach names to them. I smile tightly and nod. "I think so, though if you could all wear name tags, I'd appreciate it. Otherwise, I'm just going to call you some random name."

Levi laughs. "Most of the time, we don't know what name to answer to anyway. Our character name—which changes every two weeks—or our real name. Basically, we'll answer to anything or nothing. "

The crowd laughs. Someone—I think his name is Zak—says, "Which names? Our birth names or our stage names?"

"Do a lot of you use stage names?" I ask, taking a bite of my carrot stick.

A few people raise their hands. Zak nods. "My real name is Mike Jones. For real. Like, could you have a more basic name than that?"

"What are you using now?"

"Zak Zayson." He flutters his arms and waves jazz hands about, popping his shoulder at the same time. "I like how it zings in the mouth."

"You like lots of things that zing in your mouth," someone pipes up.

"That's what he said," Zak says with a laugh.

I can't help but join in the laughter. I glance behind me to see if Josh and the music crew are laughing too.

They're not.

Okay, so I guess Josh was right all those years ago. The actors and the musicians are sworn mortal enemies, on opposite sides of the 38th parallel. And I guess I'm on the other side of the line now.

Josh doesn't seem upset by that. In fact, if I didn't know better, I'd say he was happy to have that divide. I look again, to see him laughing at something the person next to him said. And that's when it hits me—why he looks so different. It's not the hair. It's not that his face changed as we aged. It's that he never smiles around me. I don't get to see those straight white teeth or the dimples that emerge just below the corners of his mouth as it's stretched into his trademark shit-eating grin.

I haven't even seen his shit-eating grin since I left him ten years ago.

My first instinct is to drop my head and cry, but we all know I never let myself cry. Just because I *want* to is no reason to actually do it. Instead, I try to focus on what I'm doing, right here, right now, to prevent that massive dive down into a deep, dark place inside my brain.

"I'm on the fence about a stage name," I confess, forcing myself to be present with the people at my table. "My name is, like, really terrible for a ballerina."

Jasmine shrugs. "Leslie isn't so bad. And with Leslie Odom, Jr. hitting it big, it's probably making a comeback."

"Yeah, it's the last name. Moose." I see everyone wince. "Right? I know."

"So change it."

If it was only that simple. My grandfather actually did change his last name when he moved to England to play rugby. His original last name was quite Fijian: Kaukauabulumakau. Yeah, try fitting that on the back of a jersey. The meaning was "strong cow," and his nickname quickly became Moose. When he went pro, he officially changed it. And since he, as well as my father, are legends in the rugby world, Moose it is.

On some level, I know it's just a name and one by any other would smell as sweet or whatever—but perhaps sound better. I've even thought about doing some sort of anagram of the original family name—there are certainly enough letters—but I can't bring myself to pull the trigger.

"Maybe keep it," Amy offers. "Maybe it'll make you memorable. Like I once went to a plastic surgeon whose name was Dr. Hacker. He was good, but man, I was a little terrified going in."

"Yeah, but there are always the comments about my weight and stuff because I'm not built like a typical ballerina." People can be cruel. Especially in the ballet world. Although truth be told, it wasn't even the other students as much as the parents. No one wanted to see their precious daughter upstaged by someone who looked like me.

"People are dicks," Levi says. "Trust me, sister, we know. We all know. We're like the Island of Misfit Toys here, but we're here together."

And sitting here, eating—actually eating—with these kindred spirits, for the first time in my life, I'm starting to wonder if I've been focusing on the wrong thing all along.

Maybe there's more to life than being the best?

Chapter 10: Josh

Images of Leslie dance through my brain.

Lying in bed at night, I should not be having fantasies about her. I should not be thinking about how she's in this same building, or how easy it would be to ask her if she wants to come to my room.

Hell, we wouldn't even have to sneak around like we did at camp. No worries about being caught or having our parents called. It certainly did kick up the adrenaline a notch, not like we needed any more rushing hormones.

I wonder how Mei made out with the Hamptons gig this weekend. I should probably think about her more than I do. I force myself to try and remember what she felt like.

I'm drawing a blank. When I was seeing her for gigs every weekend, or even a few times a week, it seemed like a good thing. I haven't seen her since I came up here the first week in May.

It's now the third week in June.

That doesn't bode well for our relationship.

I should probably call it off officially. Not that I need to be free for any other entanglements or anything.

Still, I open my Instagram page and type her name in the search bar. And there she is. Skimpy white bikini, mason jar cocktail in hand. "Happy in the Hamptons!" it reads, followed by more hashtags than should probably be legal. I swipe to the next picture in the series. There are about six with her in various poses. Number seven though ...

It's a selfie of her. And Mark. Kissing.

Are you kidding me?

This isn't an inadvertent post. Her social media is carefully crafted and cultivated to show what a perfect and glamorous life she leads as a lounge singer. This isn't even on her private Insta account. Oh no, this is on @meilinmusician.

Shit.

I'm not even that upset. More annoyed than anything else. I guess she doesn't need me to call it off.

And Mark? He's a total douche. What does she see in him?

Instantly, my mind flashes back to that night. Mei in the Uber. It wasn't a shared ride. It was Mark. She was going home with him instead of me.

Ten bucks says they were together before that show too.

Assholes.

You know, sometimes I wish I could date the old-fashioned way, without social media, like my parents did. I bet it was so much easier. You wouldn't have to worry about being catfished or ghosted. You wouldn't find out you're being cheated on when the rest of the world sees it.

Seriously, she's got over five thousand followers on this account.

I should be a bigger person and let it go. Except right now, I'm not. I "like" her post.

And now I wait for her to call to explain.

And I wait.

And wait some more.

This is bullshit.

I sit up and flick the light on. I need to focus on something else. I open my notebook to the empty page that's been taunting me, almost as much as Mei's Instagram post.

This ballad comes as the main character realizes that the charade she's been living is closer to reality than she realized. The protagonist, a trivial woman who goes by both the names Dawn and Honor, realizes that she's much more like her alter ego and that only in being true to this self can she be happy.

What's been the most difficult about penning this number is that this is a comedy, so this song still has to have some humor in it.

Humor, when you're down in the dumps, is a commodity in short supply.

There's a soft knock on my door, saving me from scribbling out more things that don't work.

I really should use a pencil.

"Did I wake you?" Leslie's face is freshly scrubbed and her curly hair is piled high on top of her head. She's in short shorts and a cropped T-shirt that shows a swath of bronze skin. I look at her shirt. *Do your best. Be the best. Whatever it takes.*

"Nice shirt."

She glances down. "Yeah, well, my dad thought if we were wearing it, we'd have to live it. Guess I showed him." She looks up and down the hall. "Can I come in?"

I push open the door farther, but still not moving out of the way. She slides in under my arm and then sits down cross-legged on the foot of my bed.

"Make yourself at home."

And then I wait. She doesn't say anything. I sit down in my lounge chair. Because I'm the musical director, I get my own room, which is the same size as the rooms that hold multiple cast members. As a result, I have room to trick it out with comfy furniture. Also, Grayson was getting rid of this chair and it was still perfectly good, so I totally snatched it up.

I fold my hands behind my head. Two can play this game.

"You never smile when I'm around."

I shrug, not sure what to say to that. I'm guessing she doesn't want my honest opinion.

Though in all honesty, I don't even know what I'm thinking.

"I thought you understood, but it seems like you don't."

What is she talking about? "Understood? Understood what?"

She sighs, still looking at the hands that are knotted together between her legs. "That ballet is my life. Was my life," she quickly corrects. "I told you it

91

was everything to me, and that I didn't have the time for anything else." Finally, she looks at me. "That included you too. Ballet was everything, and there was nothing left for you."

"Why didn't you say that?"

"I did. I tried. You didn't want to hear it."

"Why did you get involved with me, to begin with, if you knew it wouldn't last? Couldn't last?"

Didn't she know it was cruel to make me fall in love with her and then to take that love away? Especially when everything else in my life was taken away.

She stands up. "I wish you knew what my life was like. I thought you understood, but you didn't. Those eight weeks at STP were about the most normal time I ever had."

"Seriously? A setting like that is anything but normal. We were together twenty-four seven. The relationships are hyperintense, and it all happens in a bubble. It's so not normal."

"Was strengthening and conditioning and ballet class after ballet class? Cramming my homework in so I could get it all done before the four to five hours of class each night? I was already behind the eight ball by not being home tutored so I could take class all day. Hell, the only thing I did for fun—other than eating and going to my dad's rugby games—was to take Polynesian dance classes to appease my grandparents. So yeah, not the typical teen experience. I didn't go to football games. I practiced. I didn't go to the mall. I practiced. I didn't go to the prom. I went to auditions. I obsessed about being the best."

"But you blocked me." Now I sound like a spoiled teenager. "Who does that? We didn't even fight. The last thing you said to me was 'I love you.' And then you blocked me, probably before you even got home."

I couldn't even tell her. She still doesn't know.

"I had to. You were a distraction. And as long as that temptation was there, I knew I wouldn't be able to focus on what was important."

Those words hurt probably more than she intended.

I stand up and begin to pace. "It's nice to know I wasn't important."

Leslie collapses back on the bed. "You still don't get it. You were important. That was the problem. I couldn't afford for you to be important. It was energy I didn't have to spare."

What I hear is that I wasn't worth the energy. I don't say anything. She has no idea what she did to me.

"Okay, so you know my grandparents are from Fiji, right? Well, in Fiji, the value system is God, family, and rugby. Sometimes rugby comes before family, especially on game day. Like literally, the banks shut down when there's a game and everything stops. For me, substitute ballet for rugby. I don't know any other way. My family doesn't know any other way."

"You don't think I feel the same way about music? You don't think it's with me every moment of every day?" That I have to carry on my parents' legacy, and that my success is their success? That I'm doing this for them as much as for me?

She covers her face with her hands, still lying on her back across my bed. "It's not the same. You ... you can be a musician at any age. With any color. With any body type. I have—*had*—such a small window to shove that square peg into a round hole. So few people get to the level I got to. Even fewer succeed. Do you know what the statistics are? It's something like three-hundred thousand people try for a professional ballet job each year. Only two percent get hired. That's not a lot of people in the grand scheme of things. I thought if I just hammered away hard enough, eventually, it'd fit. But no matter what, I'm still me. I still have wide feet and round boobs and not enough skill. I'm still a square peg."

I want to be mad at her, but suddenly, I feel sorry for her. I can't imagine going through your whole life trying to fit in. I walk over to the bed, sitting down next to her. I make sure to leave some distance between us. I'm not going to be tempted into touching her.

I'm not a dick, and she's obviously hurting.

I'm still hurting.

"Maybe you need to find a different hole."

"I don't want a different hole. I want to be successful in the hole I picked."

I shake my head at the turn this conversation has taken. We need to stop talking in terms of holes. It's bringing my mind to a crude place. "And how do you define success?"

"In order to be successful, you have to be the best. And for me, that means being a professional ballerina."

"Okay, so where do you stand with that?" She auditioned for The Edison in the first place and was available at a moment's notice to come up here. I think I know what she's going to tell me, but maybe working through this will help her.

"Well, after years of training with the Five Boroughs Ballet Company, I was finally promoted to the corps de ballet last season when a freak accident sidelined several dancers."

I wince at her words. I understand how freak accidents can change a person's life.

"At the end of the season, as everyone was recovering, they released me from my contract. I'm no longer a member of FBBC. I'm officially an unemployed, has-been ballerina. I'm too old to audition anywhere else. Definitely not a professional. Definitely not the best."

"That sounds crushing." I can't imagine what it's like to be so close to your dream only to have it ripped away. Maybe someday I'll know, but I'm only starting out on that journey right now. I glance over at my notebook. Perhaps I could use a little of Leslie's focus and drive to get this finished so I can start pitching it for real.

"Yeah, and then the only thing worse than getting fired was having my parents find out. They, like, actually came to New York to fetch me to bring me back home. The call from Henderson is the only thing that prevented me from having to return to Ohio in shame."

That's not the worst thing that can happen. The worst thing is a drunk driver, so inebriated on a Sunday morning that a sixteen-year-old becomes an orphan.

I almost want to tell her this, but her pain is as real as mine is. "Is that the only reason you took the part? Because it was this or go back home?"

She nods.

I try to pull my focus back to Leslie and where she was. *Is*. "And let me guess, like all those years ago at STP, you still don't really care about being an actress."

She shakes her head slightly.

"And now?"

Abruptly, she sits up and before I know it, she's across the room at my door.

"What?" I ask.

"You don't want me to say it."

"I do. I want to hear what you're thinking." It's true. I have no idea how her mind works. Obviously.

"Josh ..." she pleads.

"Jesus, Leslie, just say it. What are you doing here?"

She takes a deep breath in as if she's about to jump off a cliff. "I'm selling out and selling myself short. I'm settling."

Her words, referring to the thing I love the most, land like a blow to the gut. She might as well be saying that anyone who ends up with me is settling.

Perhaps Mei felt the same way about me.

Leslie turns and walks out, leaving another wake of destruction in her path. If The Edison had any other options besides her, I would certainly be pounding on Grayson's door, pleading my case right now.

I only know one thing—I cannot be around her. She represents too much hurt for me, pulling me back to the worst time in my life. She's going to have to find someone else to work on music with her.

If I never see Leslie Ann Moose again, it will be too soon.

Chapter 11: Leslie

I thought talking to Josh would make me feel better. We were such fast friends at camp that I figured that bond would still be there, no matter what.

I was wrong.

I find this out as I show up for my music rehearsal on Tuesday morning. Between dance rehearsals, aerial rehearsals, and group number rehearsals, I haven't been able to focus on my song the way I should have. The way I need to. Henderson blocked me out for a good hour with Josh to hammer this out.

I sounded *bad* yesterday. Like people were actually wincing. I know I was awful.

I'm nervous about being alone with him again. I haven't spent any time with him since last Saturday when I left his room. Three days doesn't seem like a lot, but the environment here at The Edison is much like it was at camp. Josh was right—it's a bubble, which makes everything seem so much more intense.

Like I need more intense.

My stomach is in knots, thinking about the hour or two we're going to spend together. Working on music and vocals can be nearly as intimate as dancing together. And even though I'm pretty sure he's not on the same page, I yearn for that intimacy with him again.

In the ten years since we parted, I've never come close to having the feelings I did with Josh. Maybe because we started off as friends. Fast friends. Close friends. It wasn't like I was there for a romantic relationship, though plenty of the campers were.

But for the first time in my life, without the pressures of ballet, I could stay up late, talking into the dark of night while fireflies lit up the sky. I could tell him something between sessions. If we weren't actively running something, there was downtime to just sit and hang out. It wasn't like I was a lead who was in every scene. The dance numbers I was in were easy compared to what I was used to. Josh, being the virtual musical prodigy that he is, didn't need much practice time either.

I take a deep breath before entering the music room, trying to will my hand to stop shaking as it reaches for the door handle.

It's just Josh.

Except it's not Josh. It's Gloria.

"Oh." The disappointment slips out before I can catch myself. See? Not much of an actress.

"Hi to you too. Josh asked me to run this with you today."

"I'm sure he did." I drop my bag to the floor with a little more force than necessary.

"Whoa. What's up?"

"Nothing. I'm fine."

"Fine is the biggest lie. I know that fib. It was my go-to phrase. You're obviously not fine. You wanna talk about it?"

"Nope."

Gloria nods. "All right then. Just remember not to shoot the messenger here."

We run through some warm-ups and then start on my piece.

"Okay, that's sounding much better than the last time we worked on it."

"Yeah, Josh broke it down for me last week. I was hoping for some more of his magic today."

Gloria tilts her head. "For him or his magic?"

I'm pretty sure the only thing I could do to make Josh more upset with me is to air our dirty laundry for everyone here at The Edison. "He's just really good at this music stuff, and it's not my forte," I cover quickly.

I busy myself flipping through the music book. Not including my duet with Levi, I'm in four other numbers as the ensemble. It's a lot of dancing and singing to learn. I do better in the group numbers because it's not on me to carry things vocally. Still, it's not enough to coast.

That stupid "being the best" thing is really a drag sometimes.

This is helpful to work on my music and parts. Gloria is patient and kind, not to mention talented. She's got the type of voice that you just stop and listen to when she's singing. Gloria is also a good teacher, breaking down my parts in ways that are helpful. She almost makes me feel like I can do this.

"Thanks for this. I need all the help I can get," I say, packing up my book. I'm going to need to burn the midnight oil working on my vocals, not to mention my lines. We open in nine days. That's not a lot of time to put together a show of this magnitude.

Hell, I still have to fly across the stage. Multiple times. Without a mat.

Suddenly, the thirty-two fouetté sequence from *Swan Lake* doesn't seem so intimidating. I mean, not that I could do that either. In class, I only ever made it to twenty-eight turns. Once again, so close, but so far away.

"Listen, you're doing great. I know how it seems, but you've got plenty of time."

"We open next Thursday. I'm starting to feel like that scene in *Dirty Dancing* when Baby yells at Johnny because he won't show her lifts and then they go to the lake."

Gloria laughs. "I get it. I literally stepped in the week of. I know the pressure. I thought I was going to die, and that's even with the adrenaline pumping. This is like doing a triathlon every day for three weeks."

"And having to have a smile on your face while you do it."

"That's show biz, kid."

Gloria delicately puts her hand on my arm. "Leslie, if you ever want to talk about anything, I'm here. I don't know what you're going through, but ..." She looks around, clearly not knowing what to say next.

"Thanks, I'm—"

"Don't say fine," Gloria interjects. "Be honest. In this moment. Maybe for the first time. You don't have to say it out loud, but at least be honest with yourself. And consider that what you've been telling yourself all this time may not be the truth. It might be your perception rather than reality."

Gloria's words ricochet through my head. I don't know if I've ever been honest with myself. "What do you mean?"

"I have an anxiety disorder and PTSD. I didn't before the incident, but thanks to my asshole ex-boyfriend and the even bigger asshole bitch he was cheating on me with, I do now. My irrational fear was that everyone had seen me naked. Like *everyone*. I mean, the video went viral, but there are still people in the world who haven't seen it. At least I hope there are. But by then I was convinced that everyone had seen me naked. Or was conspiring to see me. That I was constantly being filmed without my consent."

"Oh God, that sounds awful."

"It was. I barely left my house. When I did, I had to freakishly scour the place for hidden cameras. It didn't matter that I never found one. I had no trust. But the person I had the least trust in was me because I'd trusted him to begin with."

As confusing as that sentence is, her words make sense. But I don't see how they apply here. We're walking over to the dorm to get some lunch. "Yeah, but that's not what's going on with me."

Gloria smiles a little. "No, but you know as well as I do that you're not fine. And also, you know you are holding onto beliefs that may or may not be true. And those beliefs are causing you pain. Now, what do you want for lunch? Let me guess—a salad."

Shame instantly floods my cheeks. How did she figure it out?

"I've gotta run to my room first. It's that time of the month, you know?" I sprint away before she can say anything else. My heart pounds in my chest. I might as well be standing in front of her naked, my inner truth exposed like that.

She should understand a little more of how that feels.

I run up the stairs and turn quickly down the hall, running squarely into Josh. It's like in the train station, except this time I don't pull up short and I do manage to knock him over.

"Oooph." He exhales as we hit the floor with a thud, my body weight slamming onto him.

I want to immediately apologize, but the rawness of my emotions is too much. I collapse down onto Josh's chest and start crying.

Sobbing, if you really want to know.

I feel his arms snake around me, lightly rubbing my back. "You're okay, Leslie."

I put my hands on the floor above Josh's shoulders and push myself up a little. "But I'm not. I'm so not. Can't you see that?"

I look into his hazel eyes, which are intently staring into my own. Probably because I have him pinned to the floor and he literally has nowhere to go.

"What are you running from? What are you afraid of?"

Myself.

I stare at him, unable to articulate my feelings.

"Jesus, Leslie. For once in your life, be honest. What are you afraid of?"

This is the second time in a few minutes someone told me to be honest with myself. Perhaps it's time to heed that advice. "I'm afraid of failing."

"Haven't you already done that?" His words are not meant to hurt. They're plain and pointed. And true. "And what happened? Did the world end?"

I shake my head.

"So you failed at becoming a professional ballerina. Most people fail at that. You should take comfort in the fact that you were good enough to make it that far."

"Good enough isn't the best."

"So what? There's more to life than being the best, especially the way you've gone about it. Maybe you were trying to be the best at ballet, but you were totally sucking at everything else. Like being a friend and girlfriend."

The word shocks me, pulling me right out of the downward spiral I was careening through. "Girlfriend? You thought I was your girlfriend?"

Josh pushes me off of him, sitting up. His breath is coming in short spurts. I can't tell if he's out of breath because I knocked the wind out of him or if he's that upset with me. "Of course I did. You meant a lot to me. I loved you. I told you that. I'd never said it to anyone before."

"Me neither. And I haven't said it to anyone since."

"I'm sure you haven't had time to."

I deserve that. "You know, I was fired like two months ago. I've had some free time. I tried dating. I don't think Tinder is the place for me."

Josh laughs, giving me a quick glance at that smile that melted my heart so long ago. He stands up and extends a hand down to me. I take it, accepting his help as he pulls me to my feet.

"I don't think Tinder is the place for most decent human beings."

I look at him for a minute, not wanting to let go of his hand. Not wanting this moment between us to end. I need to do something—anything—to preserve this tiny little bit of the thing that used to be between us.

"Josh," I blurt. "I had an eating disorder. That's why I was at camp. My parents thought if I didn't have to put on a leotard every day and be in the room with people who constantly judged me on my appearance, I'd get better. If I wasn't so focused on ballet, I'd stop obsessing about what I put in my body."

He drops my hand but doesn't step away. "Did it help?"

I bow my head, looking at my feet. I've never told anyone this before. It's a very private, very shameful thing. "I think it did. For a while at least." I raise my head to look at him again. "Because you fell in love with me. I had to be worthy of something. I carried that with me for a long time. You helped me heal."

"So knowing I loved you gave you confidence and strength and made you whole?" That muscle is tense in his jaw again.

I nod, unsure of where he's going with this.

"Then how did you think it would make me feel for you to no longer love me?"

Chapter 12: Josh

I ... I didn't think about that," she stammers.

"You didn't think about me at all."

I needed her so much, and I never crossed her mind.

"I thought about you all the time. I thought about your smile and your laugh and your hands on my body."

I don't believe you.

Her words are bringing images to my head that I want to stay dead and buried. I close my eyes, trying to will them away. Trying to will *her* away.

"Josh." She reaches out, touching my arm. "Josh, I wasn't well. I wasn't in a place to give you back what you deserved. You deserved so much more than me. I could never give you back all those things you gave me."

I shrug. "You could have tried. I needed you. I needed a friend."

After the accident, I was so lost. There was so much pain. I was convinced that Leslie would help me through it. But she wasn't there for me. She didn't care about me. But then I think about what she just told me and something in my heart breaks a little for her. She wasn't trying to hurt me. She wasn't even lashing out. She was just ... broken herself.

It's hard for broken pieces to put someone else back together.

I put my other hand over hers, sandwiching it between my arm and my palm. "Listen, it's the past. It really is. We were both kids. I'm not foolish enough to think that what we had at sixteen would last us forever or anything like that. I'm not the same person I was back then." I squeeze her hand slightly. "I'm the new and improved version."

"I'm not sure who I am, but I don't know if I can use the word 'improved' quite yet."

One more squeeze and then I drop both my hands. "You need to figure that out. You'll never be happy until you do. Now, were you coming or going from lunch?"

She gives me a watery smile. "I still need to eat. I ran out because Gloria made a comment that hit close to home. She saw through me. The eating stuff."

"Is it still an issue?" I try to remember what I've ever seen her eat. Fruits. Vegetables. Salads. A pit forms deep in my stomach. And then a pit forms on top of that because I don't want to care, but I do.

"When I get stressed and anxious, it's harder for me to control. When I'm in a good place, I do okay."

I wonder what she defines as "okay."

I sling my arm around her shoulder, steering her toward the stairs. "Well, then you should be just fine.

There's absolutely nothing to be stressed or anxious about here, now, is there? No pressure whatsoever."

I purposely try to make my tone light. The last thing she needs is my residual feelings weighing her down.

She smiles slightly. Mission accomplished.

What I do understand is this: she was in no place to be in a relationship back then, and it doesn't seem like she's evolved much either. It was just unfortunate timing for me. Leslie has a lot of healing to do. The Edison has worked wonders for a lot of people, including Gloria. I hope Leslie can start on that path while she's here.

And then it hits me. The motivation for my lead character who lives a double life. When Oscar Wilde originally wrote the play, *The Importance of Being Earnest*, it was in a very trivial way. The character creates an alter ego just because he's bored. But I know that my main character has other reasons.

She's creating the person she wants to be, rather than the person society tells her she should be. She's Leslie.

I grab a quick sandwich and rush back to my room to scribble down my ideas. This is what I needed. This eureka moment.

My phone buzzes with a text message asking where I am. *Shit*. I've got to get to rehearsal. The sandwich is largely untouched, so I grab it, shoveling it in my mouth as I take the stairs two at a time. I'm still chewing as I hit the auditorium. "Sorry," I mumble. "I was working on my—"

"Show. We know. You're always working on your show," Zak laughs. "Are we ever going to see this show or is it just some mythical creation?"

"You know, like a hetero chorus boy?" Levi pipes in.

Everyone laughs. I've got so much adrenaline rushing through me. "No, it's coming. I'm—"

"Almost done. We've heard that before." Zak nods sagely.

"No, I had a breakthrough and figured out what I was missing." Involuntarily, my eyes dart to Leslie. I pull my gaze back to Zak. "But enough about my show. Where are we with this one? I think we're working on 'From Now On' today. Gray, you ready?"

These huge ensemble numbers can take days to work out. The song ends up being over five minutes long. There are tons of transitions and layers of choreography. It's the final number in the show, so we have to pull out all the stops. The entire cast will pretty much be on the stage at some point, and Leslie will be doing aerial tricks above everyone.

We need to break down the vocals first before they try to learn the choreography. Everyone separates into their groups by classification. This is my favorite part. Teaching the separate lines and then layering them together to create powerful harmonies. I see notes weaving together like a painter mixes colors.

As excited as I am for *The Greatest Showman*, I'm even more excited to see—and hear—my vision come to life for my show. I wonder if I can get some people here to do a rough demo for me. Someone hits a note that's way off, pulling me back in.

"Let's try that again. We're looking for a D_4 on that one. I think someone hit $E\#_4$." I tap out the note on the piano a few times for the sopranos to hear.

It takes about two hours to get through the music for this song. Now it's Kori's turn to take over with choreography. I've recorded a track of the instrumentals for her to use so I don't have to play the piano the whole time. I don't mind sitting here for some of it, but I was going to use this time to run over Tabitha's number with her since she's pretty much the only person not in the finale.

It's amazing to work with someone who's this level of professional. I hope it won't be the last time. I mean, she was nervous—nervous!—about this piece, so she worked with her own vocal coach to prepare.

"I don't think we have much to do, but let's run through this a few times, just so you feel comfortable."

Tabitha smiles. She begins singing "Never Enough," a soulful, wistful ballad that has the potential to freeze the audience in its tracks. Especially the way Tabitha sings it. I'm not sure what's going on with her and Henderson, but anyone with eyes can see it. I feel as if she's singing this directly to him.

If that's the case, she should stick with it because it's working for her.

"Are you getting back in the recording studio anytime soon?" I can't help but ask. "Is there another reunion planned?"

"We haven't talked about anything, but on the other hand, we didn't talk about it last time. Callie just booked us and assumed we'd all drop everything to be there." She shrugs. "Which is basically what happened."

"Maybe you should book something and see if they all show up."

Tabitha laughs. "The best I can do is a partial reunion. I know Mandy is coming to at least one of the shows, and I think Angie will as well. Last I heard, Callie's in England, so I don't think she'll be flying in. We're not important enough."

I break into one of the Sassy Cats' songs, and Tabitha immediately starts singing along. I realize she's a register off from me, so I adjust. She smiles at the fix.

"How do you know that music? I mean, it's not generally something you hear at a piano concert."

Sheepishly, I lift my shoulders and then let them casually fall. "I dunno. I can just hear things and play them. I can tell what the notes are."

"Like you hear a note and know that it's a G or D or whatever?" Tabitha wrinkles her nose. "Okay, like, I can't really read music. I mean, I have an idea what that note sounds like when I see it on the paper, but I don't know the names of them. So if you mention them in abstract, I pretend to know what you're talking about, but I don't. I'm like the worst singer ever."

"Obviously you're not. Here, sing this." I play a note. She matches it perfectly. "Now go up a full step."

She does.

"Now come down a half-step."

She does that as well.

"Bring it down a full register."

Once again, she nails it.

"Now up."

I take my hands off the keys. "You may not know the names of the notes you're singing, but you know how to sing. You have a nice range and excellent control. I'd say you have relative pitch. You may not know the names of the notes, but you know the notes. I'm sorry, but I cannot dub you the worst singer ever. In fact, I'm much worse of a singer than you."

Tabitha laughs, sitting down on the piano bench next to me. "I doubt that."

"No, it's true. I'm a musician. Have you ever wondered why I don't sing the notes I want you to sing? I play them on the piano. My voice is not great. Especially not considering the wealth of vocal talent in the room." I waggle my eyebrows.

"How did you get started with music? Like, how did you find out you had talent? I'm guessing you didn't go to an open call like I did."

"Nah. My mom was a music teacher and my dad was in a jazz band. I was born into it. Also, my mom realized I had perfect pitch when I was like five, so the writing was on the wall from that time."

"What's perfect pitch?"

"I can identify any note by hearing it. I don't need a reference note or anything. You need the reference note and then can go from there. I can just hear a note and identify it."

"So, like any note?"

"Any note. Any key."

Tabitha cocks her head. "That's so cool. I've never heard of it before."

"It's also called absolute pitch. I read one time that like one in ten thousand people have it, so it's not that common. I mean, when I was at Berklee, I'd say like ten percent of my class had it, but we're all music nerds."

"You went to UC Berkeley? I love Northern California. We played there on tour when we were just starting out. It's a super fun college."

I smile at her error. Most people outside the performing arts industry would make the same assumption. "No, Berklee College of Music, in Boston. I'm from New Hampshire originally. Berklee's the best in the Northeast, second only to Juilliard, probably. John Mayer and Quincy Jones went there too."

"Well, aren't you the musical genius?" She laughs. "I may need you to teach me how to read music someday." She leans in, whispering in my ear, "I'm thinking I might like to do this theater thing."

"I think you'll do great at whatever you want to do. But if you want help breaking down the music, my door's always open."

Tabitha stands up and bops me on the nose with her finger. "You're adorable. And smart too. Some girl or guy needs to snatch you up."

"Girl," I say. "And maybe someday. I just found out the girl I was sort of seeing is shacking up with our bass player. She posted a pic on Insta, so I'm guessing she doesn't find me as adorable."

Tabitha shrugs. "Her loss. Totally. Because mark my words, someday Josh, you're going to be a big star. And when that happens, everyone you've ever met will come out of the woodwork claiming to be your best friend. But if they weren't good friends to you before, they're not really looking to be your friend now."

She reaches into her bag and pulls out her phone. Tabitha slides in close, holding her arm up, and snaps a selfie of the two of us at the piano. "I'm gonna tag you in that. Let her eat her heart out now."

I mull over Tabitha's words. I mean, I don't think I have to worry about being a star just yet, but it gives me perspective. Who do I have in my life that is my friend now? D'von probably. Definitely not Mark or Mei. Maybe some people from here? Grayson and Henderson are a possibility.

Then my mind wanders back to Leslie. I don't think she has enough reserves to even give to a friendship right now.

And that makes me sad.

Chapter 13: Leslie

I always thought being honest with someone about my issues would lead me down a dark—er—shame spiral. Yet in the days since my conversation with Josh, somehow, I feel lighter.

Talk about irony.

It's the closing night for *Kiss Me, Kate*, which means most of the cast and crew are scrambling. It also means we're in the home stretch for the opening of *The Greatest Showman* in four short days.

Gah.

While that's on my mind, I've got something else occupying more space. As the audience is piling into the theater, I text Gloria, asking if she can talk. A few minutes later, I'm sitting in the kitchen of Grayson's house. As a rule, the cast doesn't hang out at the Keene's house, but Gloria assured me this was okay.

She hands me a cup of tea and then curls up on the chair to my right, folding her petite little legs under her in an effortless way.

I look down at the thin brown liquid, working up the courage to say what I came here to say. Finally, I look back up. "I'm sorry, this is hard."

Gloria nods. "I get it. I'm here whenever you're ready."

I take a deep breath. It's now or never. "I think I need help. You said you moved here to work with a therapist. Do you think they can help me?" The wind rushes out of me as if I'd just moved a thousand-pound weight.

Gloria pulls out her phone. "I'll text Malachi right now, though there's a good chance he's at the show."

Relief crashes into me, the glimmer of hope on the horizon. "Do you think he can help me?"

"I think if you're ready, then yes." She smiles at me. "I've done a lot of therapy over the years with a lot of different therapists. Malachi specializes in Eye Movement Desensitization and Reprocessing— EMDR—for PTSD, but I'm fairly confident he's a good cognitive behavior therapist as well." She reaches over, putting her hand on mine. "Congratulations on taking the first step."

I pull my mouth into a tight line. "Why do I have the feeling it's only step one of a marathon?"

"Because it is. But you'll never cross that finish line until you start. You're officially one step closer to the end now." Now it's Gloria's turn to take in a deep breath. "The one thing is that his sessions can be kind of pricey. I'm not sure if he accepts insurance. The EMDR is not covered, but regular therapy might be."

Crap. That's a layer I hadn't considered.

After leaving Gloria, I walk around the grounds at The Edison. The music floats out into the warm summer air, speckled with sounds of laughter and applause. This really is a special place to be.

Okay, I know what I have to do.

"Hi, Mom."

"Leslie! What's wrong? Are you hurt? You never call unless something's wrong. You only text."

I sit down on a bench. "Nothing's wrong. I'm fine." The lie flows from my mouth without any effort; a reflex so skillfully smooth at this point. "No, wait, that's not true. I'm not fine."

"Is it your Achilles again? Are you using the Tiger Balm?"

I live on Tiger Balm. And Biofreeze. And Ben Gay. Hell, my natural scent is old folk medication at this point.

"No, Mom, it's not my Achilles. I'm not dancing en pointe right now, so it's actually pretty good. Everything else is sore from the aerial work, but it's a good sore."

I realize how easy it is to slide into the conversations about tangible injuries that can be healed with balms and stretching. Maybe even a little surgery. But there's no quick fix for the rest of me, and it's time to open that wound so the healing can begin.

"Mom, I'm doing well at the theater here, but I'm not okay. I haven't been okay in a long time. I think you know that."

"But you said you were eating."

Again she resorts to the tangible. Food is easier to focus on than a messed-up mind and other deep-seated issues. Like my race.

"I'm trying to. But do you know why I restrict my food?"

"Because of those bitches in ballet class." My mom rarely swears. On the other hand, her assumption disappoints me. It's so much easier to blame someone else.

"I mean, they didn't help. Sometimes, people were mean. But people can always be mean. I didn't restrict food because someone told me to."

"Then why would you be so unhealthy? Don't you know how bad that is for you?"

I roll my eyes, safe through the phone where my mom can't see. "The meanest person of all is me, Mom. I'm very mean to myself. But I don't want to be anymore. I want to be able to love myself."

"What kind of granola crap are they feeding you up there? You are who you are."

I don't think she's trying to be obtuse. She's from a long line of work-the-earth farmers who just plowed forward—literally—no matter what. Even though she's never tilled the soil or milked a cow in her life, that mentality is ingrained in her.

"I don't like who I am. And I want to change that. I'm going to go to therapy, but I might need help paying for it. I'm working and getting paid here for this show, though I don't think it will be enough to cover it all."

The other end of the phone is silent for a while. Finally, I hear her voice, thick with tears. "You know we love you."

"I know, and I need to feel that for myself."

"What don't you like about yourself?"

"Aw, Mom, the list is too long and I don't have enough cell phone battery to cover all of it. Can I ask you one thing though? Will you still love me if I'm not the best?"

"Of course, honey. How can you even say that?" My dad's voice startles me.

"Mom, did you put me on speaker?"

"Of course. You never call. It had to be important."

My dad speaks up again. "We'll always love you. You know that."

I can no longer hold back the question that's been eating through my soul all these years. "Then why all the emphasis on being the best?"

It's my dad's turn to take over. "You know the Fijian people are very proud."

"Yes, Dad. You've told me a million times. Being Fijian is the best thing ever." I roll my eyes again. Maybe I should speak to my parents on the phone more often. It's quite satisfying to be able to be snarky without them knowing.

"But when you are back home on the island, there's a part of the culture that's not so great."

"It's the cannibalism thing, isn't it?" Yes, the myths are true. Some tribes of native Fijians used to have a more … protein-heavy… diet.

"No, Leslie. It's the crab mentality."

"Huh?" He's lost me.

"We are like crabs piled in a bucket. One can try to escape, and probably could, but the others pull him back down. It's like if they all can't get out, then none should. As great as our people are, it's a negative way of thinking. The only way out of that bucket is through rugby or education. My parents did not want me getting trapped in the bucket, pulling down and being pulled down. Excelling in rugby or education was the only way to stay out of the bucket altogether."

"And Meri took the education route." She's a Ph.D. biomedical researcher and will probably cure cancer. Even at the age of twenty-eight, she's quickly climbing to the top in her field. She wakes up being the best. She doesn't even have to try. Not that I'm bitter or anything. "I did neither education nor rugby. I'll never get out of the bucket."

"You were never in the bucket. We wanted to make sure you were never trapped in there to begin with."

Except that's where I've been my whole life. Nature versus nurture at its finest.

I need help to climb out. I'm done with my own negative thoughts being the other crabs that pull me back down.

"So, I'm not going to be a professional ballerina. That's done." While saying these words hurt, there's an odd sense of relief.

"Did you do your best?" my dad asks.

And there it is, the feeling of inadequacy—my constant companion—is back. I want to scream, "Of course I did my best!" but self-doubt, inadequacy's BFF, is there, whispering to me that *maybe* I could have tried a bit harder and that would have made all the difference.

"I ... I think so," I answer quietly.

"Either you did or you didn't," my dad says bluntly. "Did you do your best?"

A montage of my life floats through my brain. All the hours upon hours of rehearsal. The injuries, the bleeding feet. The pain ... everywhere. Practicing combinations in my kitchen. Practicing steps in my shower. Running through variations in my head while I was trying to fall asleep at night. No social life. No boyfriend. No fun.

No Josh.

"I gave it all I had to give."

"Then there's nothing more you could have done. You should be pleased with your efforts and how far you've come. Not many people make it as far as you did."

"And Leslie," my mom chimes in, "remember that you're a beautiful dancer. I've always loved to watch you. A big part of that enjoyment was knowing the joy it brought you."

I think about what my parents said. I can't imagine not dancing. I need that movement in my life. But I'm not sure that "joy" is how I'd describe it. The feelings are too complex to be distilled down to "joy."

"I wish we could see you in this show," Mom laments.

Tickets were sold out weeks before I was brought in. Everyone wants to see Tabby Cat.

"I know. I'm going to see if I can get permission to record at least my main number so I can send it to you." I take a deep breath. As long as I'm ripping off the Band-Aid ...

"So the other show I'm in here later in the summer ..."

"Yes," Mom says eagerly. "Tell me about that. We're definitely going to get tickets and come out to see you."

The pit's back in my stomach, though not as deep as it used to be. We've had some breakthroughs. They'll accept this.

"I'm the understudy for the lead. Not the actual lead."

There's silence on the line.

"Oh," my mom finally says. "What happened?"

I shrug, not that they can see it through the phone. "I don't know." I don't. Was it my turnout? My singing voice? My read? Is the other person a better dancer? Suddenly, I have to know. "You know what, I'm going to find out."

I disconnect from my parents, marching over to The Edison offices in the front of the theater. Henderson's in there, working on the computer. I knock slightly. He looks up and tips his head to the side, indicating I should come in.

"Howzit going, Leslie?"

Nervously I sit down on the edge of the chair. Henderson doesn't seem like the friendliest of sorts. He's not mean, just ... grumpy ... most of the time. He's still clacking away on his keyboard. "I'm okay. I ... I have a weird question to ask you."

I think I see an eye roll, which is sort of his trademark facial expression. "Sup?"

Inhaling deeply, I steel myself to start. "So you cast me as the understudy for Lise. Why?"

"Why did I give you a part?" He furrows his brow.

"Why understudy? Why not the lead? Why was I the second choice?"

Henderson stops typing. He pinches the bridge of his nose for a moment before looking up at me. "Yeah, sorry 'bout that."

"What?"

"I reckon you don't know me well, but I hate drama."

"You're literally in the drama field."

"Yes, I know. But I hate the drama that goes along with it. The high-maintenance divas who complicate everything for everyone, that sort of thing. I don't like conflict and confrontation. When you came in and couldn't figure out your own name, I decided I didn't want to deal with your drama. On the other hand, you had the talent, so if anything happened, I wanted you to do the part."

I blink slowly, trying to process what he said. "You didn't cast me because I was still working on my stage name?"

"Also because that's when the story broke about Tabitha coming here, and we were figuring that out. I *may not* have been focusing on auditions as I should have. Sorry."

I knew he wasn't paying attention.

But also, what does this mean?

"So it was nothing with my abilities or talent?" I need to hear him say it.

"Not really. You would have been good as Lise." Henderson casually shrugs. "Seeing how you work, I should have cast you."

In some ways, this is worse to hear. I can't imagine telling this to my parents. My parents ...

"Can you let me do one show? My parents want to come out from Ohio and see me."

Henderson nods. "Not opening or closing, but otherwise tell me what day they want and it's yours."

I stand up and turn to leave.

"Leslie?"

"Yes?"

"I'm sorry, and I do think you should use a stage name. Let me know because programs are going to the printer tomorrow morning."

Great. I'm right back to where I started.

Chapter 14: Josh

She seems different.

I'm trying not to notice, but I can't help it.

It's like she's standing a little bit taller. Maybe moving a little bit freer. Smiling a little bit more.

It's Monday. *Kiss Me, Kate* is officially in the books, and we're striking the set today. The crew will be feverishly building the set for *Showman*, and then rehearsals will start in earnest, running the entire show for the first time.

Normally we have four days until opening, but because we've added the extra show on Thursday, we're at T minus 3.

We are so not ready.

"I need help," Leslie stands up and announces to the cast and crew, who are all sluggishly slumped over the breakfast table, nursing their coffees. "I need to come up with a stage name. Like now. Or do I even bother? Is my name okay?"

"You need a stage name," Levi answers, not even looking up from his coffee. "You cannot be a ballet dancer named Moose. No one will take you seriously."

We'd talked about the name thing at camp all those years ago. She had a lot of pride in the name because her grandfather and father were famous athletes or something. But Levi's right. The name's not right for the stage.

"Are you keeping Leslie?" Braedyn asks.

I stay focused on my bowl of cereal, pretending not to listen. It's not like I have a stake in this. It's not like I care.

Yet, I care. She should keep Leslie.

"I think so?" she says hesitantly. "I want to. I was named after Leslie Caron. What do you think?"

"Toss it all. Go with something totally different," Amy suggests.

Marcelina adds, "Do you have any names from your heritage? Something that really stands out and pops?"

This should be good. Most people don't know anything about Fiji. Hell, I didn't know anything about it until I met Leslie. What I did learn is that the names are long and have a lot of vowels. I mean, I thought deChambeau had a lot of vowels, but the French have nothing on the Fijians. I'm guessing that would not be a good direction for her to go in.

I glance up to see Leslie watching me, a questioning look in her eye.

"You want a name people can pronounce," I say. "What about Leslie Ann Layne?"

"Leslie Layne," she says slowly, trying it out.

There are murmurs of approval throughout the room.

A wide smile spreads across her face. I grin back. I can't help it. I haven't seen that smile the entire time she's been here.

And I gave her that.

The moment passes and someone mentions the time. We have to get to work. Everyone refills their coffees and juices, grabbing their bags before trekking over to the theater.

"Thanks," Leslie says, falling in step with me. I'm walking with Don and Jen, two of the other band members. They glance from Leslie to me and back again. We might be adults now, but there's still a separation between the actors and the musicians. Don and Jen slow their pace, letting Leslie and me walk ahead.

"Still the 38th parallel?" she asks, looking back at my pit bandmates.

"Apparently. See? I told you you were a rule breaker."

"I'm still not. I'm still just someone who works hard and tries to play by the rules." She's quiet for a minute. "I feel like changing my name is breaking the rules."

"You gotta do what feels right for you." That's my advice on most things. I think gut instinct is a very underrated commodity, and that most people don't listen to theirs nearly enough.

Like right now, mine is saying I should give her a second chance, but my brain is reminding me about how she abandoned me at the absolute worst time in my life.

My brain wins.

"I gotta talk to Don and Jen about something." I start to slow my pace to drop back. "See you later."

There's an awkward moment where she stops walking altogether and then we practically run into her.

"What's with her?" Jen asks once Leslie's out of earshot. "Is she trying to kiss up to you or something?"

"Trying to kiss him is more like it. Do you see the way she looks at Josh?" Don jests.

"What are you talking about? You must be smoking something good. She's just another needy actress. You know how they are."

"Mark my words. She's got a thing for you, Josh," Don doubles down.

"Everyone has a thing for Josh. He just doesn't know it. Hell, you could probably even turn me," Jen quips.

I raise my eyebrows. "Really? Let's go." I jerk my head in the direction of the dorms, trying to call her bluff. Jen and her partner Bev are two of my pit band members. And there's no way in hell I could turn her, as if such a thing actually existed.

Jen laughs. "Oh, Josh. If only you didn't have a penis."

Don nearly chokes laughing. "I think that may be my favorite quote of the summer. It definitely goes in the book."

To keep us sane, as well as laughing our asses off, the musicians keep a notebook of the hilarious things that are said all summer. At the end of the season, someone types it up and sends it out. It's a nice memento and guaranteed to bring a smile to even the darkest of days.

We do have a lot of fun here. And I haven't felt that since Leslie arrived. She's cramping my good time.

We've reached the theater, so I hold the door open for my fellow musicians. I think I'm in the clear as we make it to the pit and begin setting up our instruments. Jen can't let this go though. "I see her looking at you. I can see it in her eyes. There's something there."

"You think?" It doesn't make sense that Leslie would be interested in me. She's the one who ended things. Cold turkey, I might add. But who knows? Jen might be a good judge of this.

"Definitely. Why? You interested in her?"

This is a question I do not know how to answer. "You know, she's an actress. There's a lot of drama there."

Don sighs. "Now you're starting to sound like Henderson. And look at him! He's always been above this, but you know he's totally fooling around with Tabitha."

It's pretty obvious, even though they think they're being sly. I mean, Henderson can't tear his eyes away from her, for starters.

Shit. Is that how I am with Leslie? Is that how she is with me?

It's not like I care that people know. I mean if there was anything to know, it wouldn't bother me that others knew. I'm not trying to hide my feelings from the cast and crew. I'm trying to hide them from myself. I don't want to have them. If I had them at all. Which I don't.

Obviously.

I don't want to give her that power over me again. I gave it to her once, and she showed me she didn't deserve it. I'm not sure she ever will.

Jen keeps pushing. "I think you should go for it, Josh. You don't have as much fun as you should. Live a little."

And die a little too.

"You know I don't really have time. I'm working on—"

"We know. Your show," Don says with a distinctly exasperated tone. "Unless we see it soon, I'm going to decide there's not actually a show, and you're using it as an excuse to avoid talking to girls."

"Maybe you need to get a little to get your creative juices flowing," Jen chides.

This conversation is about to take a decidedly dirty turn, so I change the subject. "Have you guys reviewed the music? Any questions? We're going to start right at the overture and see how far we can get through before the actors need us. Also, are we placing bets?"

Sometimes, the rehearsals can run long. We make wagers to see when some of the more frequently used expressions make their first appearances. It makes for a more interesting time. Blaze, our drummer, whips out a notebook and scrawls down Grayson and Henderson's most uttered phrases. We then take turns signing up for when we think we'll hear them, accompanied by a few dollars each.

Betting always makes it more fun.

"Enough of that. We've got to get through some of this before they call us." I encourage the band to take up their instruments.

The pit band has a small window of time to actually practice the full score before we're accompanying the singers. Most of the band is pretty skilled, but it's still nice to put it all together before we add the singing.

And technically, we're an orchestra because we have strings, but no one refers to us that way. Our group is about twelve musicians, including myself. I'm usually accompanying on piano, as well as directing, so I do most of my conducting with my eyebrows.

It's a talent.

This week is going to be long and arduous, but it's my favorite week. There will be moments of panic and despair, yet everything will come together. It's hard to describe the feelings of exhilaration during those moments when we take our places in the pit and start those first notes.

There will never be a drug that can replicate that high.

It's the feeling that keeps me going. That kept me going after my parents died. My dad, especially, understood. A day without music is like trying to breathe without air.

I don't recommend it.

That's what I need to focus on now. The music.

Which is not sounding the best as we do our first run-through. Yikes.

I take a deep breath in and slowly let it out. I can see from the look on Grayson's face that he's trying to squash the same feelings of panic. So what that it's Monday and we open on Thursday.

Henderson steps over to me. "This is a bloody nightmare."

"It's always darkest before the dawn."

Henderson rolls his eyes. "Fix it, Josh. We can't go on like this."

"This is the first run-through. It's bound to be rough."

"This wasn't rough. I reckon it's a right disaster."

"Let's do notes, and then we'll try again."

The run time is supposed to be about two hours and forty-five minutes, not accounting for the intermission. We aren't even doing it full out with set changes, and it took us almost three and a half hours.

"First note," Henderson bellows. "You have to learn your lines. Off book and on cue."

It's probably Henderson's favorite direction to give. I see Blaze glancing at his notebook. "Tim," he mouths.

Dammit.

Then I start listening to Henderson's notes. He's saying Leslie's name. A lot. Even though I vowed not to look at her, I can't help but glance, just to see how she's handling this.

Her face is devoid of all expression. It's like she's a corpse, standing there. She looks pale and blank.

Oh shit.

Chapter 15: Leslie

Queen, you gotta take this in stride. It's not the end of the world."

Except it pretty much is.

I am a complete and total failure. I'm not even being dramatic or down on myself this time. I totally blew it in our first run-through. The second wasn't much better. I think I remembered three more lines and hit two more notes correctly. Other than that … yikes.

Levi tries to comfort me, much like he tried to carry me throughout our two run-throughs. We're on round number three—going on hour twelve of rehearsal—and I want to crawl in a hole and never come out again.

"I'm the worst one here," I whisper. "And I'm not even saying that for attention. I'm so not up to par, it's not even funny."

My brain has become a massive sieve, letting everything I'm supposed to remember slide through. I'm used to knowing the choreography for entire ballet productions. I could do it in my sleep. But now, I'm so freaked out about remembering my lines and how to sing that I can't even do a basic châiné turn without tripping on my own two feet.

I bet Henderson regrets calling me in. They probably could have called someone in off the street and had better results. I say as much to Levi.

"Yeah, I don't think so. You're rough today. Tomorrow will be better."

"I don't think it can be any worse."

Levi puts his arm around me. I lean my head on his shoulder, wishing it was someone else's arm. But still, the environment here is so supportive. I keep waiting for the claws to come out or for someone to push someone else down a flight of stairs or something. I certainly never felt this kind of warmth or acceptance in the FBBC.

"Come on. Let's go to the rehearsal room. They're breaking down Tabitha and Marcelina's songs right now. I'm not sure they're going to get back to us tonight anyway."

As Levi and I head out of the auditorium, I catch Josh's eye. He gives me a tight-lipped smile. It's one of the few that's been directed at me the entire time I've been here.

What's it supposed to mean? Was it encouraging? Was he laughing at me? Is he thinking that I deserve to make a fool of myself because I made a fool of him?

"Now that's some serious eye lovin'." Levi links his arm through mine.

Shit. He caught me.

"Huh? I don't know what you're—"

"Seriously, queen, do not pull that on me. I saw the way you were looking at him."

"There were no looks. Who are you even talking about?"

"He's super cute, but totally focused on his music. Somebody makes a pass at him every year, but as far as I know, he's never bitten. Trust me, most of us have tried to be bit. Oooh, can you imagine those deliciously straight teeth sinking into your skin?"

I don't even have to imagine. I had a hickey on my bottom for a week after I left camp.

Of course, it's not like I can say that to Levi. Levi might be my biggest ally here, but he's also a tremendous gossip.

Josh would probably kill me if it ever got out that we'd been involved before. Hell, he hasn't even admitted to previously knowing me. I'm following his lead. This is his home, not mine.

"Okay, what do you want to work on?"

"Everything?"

"Queen, it's ten o'clock at night. Imma need some beauty sleep up in here pretty soon. What's your biggest problem?"

Everything.

I think for a moment. "Putting the dancing and singing together. Like, I know the steps. I know the songs. I'm just not at the point where I can do them at the same time."

"Okay, then let's do our song. Really sing it out. It's just the two of us here, so there's no pressure."

This place—it's like every single person here wants every other person to be a success. It's like the opposite of the bucket of crabs.

Hell, for my mental health alone I should stay here.

Of course, after my performance tonight, I doubt Henderson will ever cast me again.

Levi and I make it through the number with choreography and singing several times before my arms finally give out.

"I'm spent. I don't have any more in my tank." I flop back on the mat.

Levi takes a long pull from his bottle. "Queen, you are a beast, and I mean that in the most complimentary way. I've never worked this hard." He lifts his arm up in the air and flexes. "Look at these guns. My arms are never this cut. And speaking of seriously sexy arms, have you seen Josh's? Sometimes he wears these old T-shirts with the sleeves cut off. It's heaven." Levi starts fanning himself.

We both startle when we hear the throat clearing. I only have the strength to lift my head up off the mat. Levi stands up. "If it isn't Mr. Gun Show himself." Levi passes by Josh and then turns back to me. He mouths "eye lovin'" in that exaggerated way of his before leaving the rehearsal space.

My head flops back down. I'm too tired for this. To hear anything Josh has to say.

"You okay? That got a little brutal there for a while."

I cover my eyes with the back of my arm. "A *little* brutal?"

"It was awful. I came to check on you."

"I'm not that bad. I don't know what happened."

Josh lies down next to me. "I know you're not that bad."

"Something in my brain short-circuited when I had to put it all together. Apparently, I'm not a triple threat. I'm a one-at-a-time threat."

Josh chuckles. "Les, remember, everyone here has already been in three shows this season. It's a grueling schedule, and it takes a while to get used to it."

"What if I don't have the time to get used to it?"

He looks at his watch. "You've got like sixty-seven hours until the curtain goes up. That's plenty of time."

Now I want to vomit.

Josh pulls back. "The cast does this all the time. They're used to it. You'll get used to the pace too."

I think about what he's saying. "Tabitha wasn't in other shows, and she's up there nailing it."

"She has one song and a reprise. She's not in any of the group numbers. She has some lines to learn. No dancing. Certainly no aerial work, which is a totally new skill for you. And let's face it, she's basically playing herself, so she doesn't even really have to act. You have to be in love with Levi. That takes some acting."

I smile. "Don't dis my boy. He's been great with me."

"Levi is great. Totally great. But it's not like there's any natural chemistry there."

Like between us.

"That's why it's called acting." *Duh.* "I'm going to get this. I swear."

"I know you will."

I think about that. If Josh has faith in me, then it'll be okay, right? "Do you think everyone else feels the same way?"

"Here's how it goes, every show. Someone has a bad rehearsal. Then the next day, someone else botches their stuff. People forget lines. They miss marks. Sometimes, that even happens during shows. Did you know that during *Wicked*, there are all these safety precautions that have to be in place for Elphaba to fly during 'Defying Gravity?' For some reason or another, it's not that uncommon for one of the things not to go right. They call those the no-fly shows. And that's Broadway. It happens."

"So basically, the moral of this pep talk is shit happens?"

Another meme for my Cricut.

Josh grins. "Pretty much. And today, you were in the shitter. I'm sure tomorrow will be better."

"I think it's already tomorrow, and I don't feel any better."

Josh stands up and reaches down to me. I take his hand, letting him pull me to my feet. My appendages feel like Jell-O. "Go up to your room, drink plenty of water, meditate, and go to sleep. You need to relax and not think about any of this. Morning will be here before you know it."

We head for the door, Josh turning the lights off behind us. The building is dark. I grab onto Josh's arm, if only not to trip over anything. We finally get to the exterior door, stepping out into the velvety black of the night.

"Sixty-seven hours?"

Josh turns to face me, our bodies close enough that I can feel the heat between us. Without thinking, I lean into him, wrapping my arms around his body. I rest my cheek on his collarbone, sighing deeply. His arms encircle me, holding onto me as I'm holding onto him.

This feels right. It feels good. It—

Abruptly, Josh pushes me back. "I think you're all right from here. See you in the morning."

And with that, he walks away as I stand there, watching him go.

I thought for a moment he had forgiven me. That he understood why I did what I did. That maybe, we could try again.

Standing in the dark, all by myself, I know I was wrong.

Chapter 16: Josh

Last night was close. So close. Too close.

I cannot let that happen again.

I meant well. I really did. But the road to hell is paved with good intentions, and Leslie Ann Moose is my own personal hell.

Still, I feel bad that I left her standing like that all alone. You know, how she left me. I didn't do it in an eye-for-an-eye way or anything. It was more because if I stood there holding her for one second longer, I was going to do something supremely stupid.

Like kiss her.

I mean, how we started was somewhat stupid to begin with.

"What are we doing tonight?" Leslie was stretched out on the bed in my dorm room, as she was any time she wasn't in rehearsal. Chrissy hadn't gotten any friendlier in the four weeks since camp had started, so Leslie had practically moved in with me. My roommate, George, was not amused.

"I think there's another bonfire. S'mores and the works."

Leslie sighed. "Are you serious? For real?"

"What else are we supposed to do? It is a camp, you know. We're lucky they're not making us climb things and whittle wood during the day." I went to Boy Scout camp once when I was nine. It was traumatic.

"But we bonfire like every other night. And then there are the sing-alongs, and you know that's not my thing. What do the other musicians do when all the actors are showing each other up with their vocals?"

That was easy. "Mostly sneak off into the woods and hook up. You've seen American Pie, right? This is basically band camp."

"Really?" That got her attention. Leslie sat straight up, clutching my pillow. "All the band members are getting freaky with each other? What about you? Who are you getting it on with?" She threw my pillow at me. Lucky for me she had a terrible arm and I caught the pillow.

"Um, no one. I befriended you, so I'm spending all my time with you. Duh." I lobbed the pillow back to her. "What are the thespians doing? Who's hooking up with who ... because you know it's happening."

She shrugged. "I don't know. I mean, I know people are, but I'm not really in with them. You know, I'm over here, sleeping with the enemy." She hurled the pillow again. This time, I barely caught it before it beaned me in the head.

"Except you're not. We're just friends. Right?" This conversation was starting to take a turn, but I had no idea where it was going to go. I mean, you'd have to be dead not to find Leslie hot and sexy. But I was her only friend here at STP. As much of a stupid and horny teen as I was, even I recognized that you don't mess with a friendship like that. I threw the pillow back to her.

"Maybe we should hook up or fool around or whatever." Her words stunned me so much that I sat there as the pillow nailed me right in the head.

"Say what now?" I finally squeaked out.

"Well, like, all I do back home is ballet. I don't have time to date or anything. And let's face it, most of the boys that I do know from class have no interest in me. And the ones who might have been around the block so many times it's gross."

"Okay, but what does that have to do with me?" I'm confused. Leslie had firmly friend-zoned me on day one. Day two actually, probably in response to the friend zone I put her in on day one.

"Why don't we mess around? You know, just for fun. Frankly, I've never really done anything, and I'm afraid with my life the way it is, I'll never get the chance before I'm old."

Even at sixteen, I realized that people found me attractive. I'd been hit on before. This was, without a doubt, the worst I'd ever heard. "So you're saying that I'm your only chance to not die a virgin? And not because you're attracted to me, but because I have the right parts and you don't want to go to the bonfire?"

She blushed deeply, her bronze skin taking on a ruddy tone. "What I meant was—shit—you're not bad to look at and we're already friends so why not?"

I stood up and walked over to her. I grabbed her hands and pulled her up to a standing position. "What happens tomorrow?"

"We go back to being friends."

As I looked into her brown eyes, I knew that would be impossible. I knew we were crossing a line that we'd never be able to uncross. That bell would be rung forever. A small voice way down in the recesses of my brain asked if I should say no. I ignored that voice.

And then I kissed her.

We never did go back to being friends. She became my everything until the moment I became her nothing.

The memories assault me, even though I'm trying not to let them in. I realize it seems foolish to still be thinking about a teen love affair all these years later. If things had ended any other way, I might be able to move on. To laugh it off even.

But I can't because of my parents. There's no way for me to separate my emotions of the two events from each other. They're one big mess of suck in my brain.

And I don't have the time for this right now. We've got about sixty hours until we open, and there's not a moment to waste. Run-through number one is rough. Number two shows some improvement. Number three has Henderson screaming and losing his shit.

It's par for the course.

I've never been in a show that didn't follow this pattern. Leslie's doing better, but she's not quite there yet. Henderson doesn't yell at her—thank God. Anyone with eyes can see how hard she's working.

Her confidence on the silks and lyra is growing, especially now that she's no longer using a mat.

It is stunning to watch her dance, whether it's on land or as she's soaring through the air. I don't know who the yahoos in charge of her ballet company were, but they were foolish to let her go.

Her harmonies still need some work though.

Damn.

I have to pull her aside and help her with them. I would for anyone else. I can't let my job integrity suffer because I don't want to be alone with her.

"Les, let's go over the harmonies and your belts." I pick up my music book and head toward the rehearsal room.

"That bad?" she asks.

"Not bad, just not there yet."

"This show is like one big massive f-u to my ego, you know? I had to get over the fact that being here isn't settling in the first place. Now, I'm the worst one here."

"Not the worst. You simply have some work to do. I would say if you had started when everyone else did, and you didn't have to take the time to learn the aerial stuff, you would have been fine. I think for *An American in Paris* in a few weeks, you'll be fine. The ballet technique is second nature to you, while a lot of the ensemble will have to work harder at that. So remember that when we get there." I sit down at the piano.

She nods at me to start.

"When you go for that belt on 'possible,' really pull from your diaphragm. That's where your power is coming from."

We run through her harmonies and belts, and she nails them. Of course, she's standing here, and not flipping and spinning. "You've got this. You can totally sing. You do have the chops. It's just the dancing and aerial work that's tripping you up."

"Someone once told me that anyone can be taught to sing."

"Yes, but not everyone ends up sounding like you. You must have had a very skilled teacher."

She slides onto the piano bench next to me. "He was so incredibly skilled, in so many ways."

I look at her, trying to suppress my grin. Why does it have to be so easy between us? "He wasn't working with a blank canvas, you know. His pupil was—*is*—talented."

We both break the eye contact that's getting a little too strong. Leslie rests her head on my shoulder. "When—*if*—I get through this, can you give me another chance?"

Tilting my head to rest on her, I close my eyes and feel as if she punched me in the gut. It would be so easy to say yes. So much of me wants to give her that chance.

But at the end of it all, I still don't think I'll ever be able to trust her again.

I stand up. "I'm sorry, but we can't go back. And even if we could, I don't want to."

I'm a liar. I want to.

I just can't.

Chapter 17: Leslie

A little heartbreak never hurt anyone, right? I mean I already feel as if I'm dying, but so much hurts physically and mentally that a little emotional anguish is just like sprinkles on my pain sundae.

Mmm ... sundae.

When this is all over, I'm going to bury my feelings in a big huge ice cream sundae, complete with all the toppings and plenty of whipped cream. I haven't had one in years, and I'm done depriving myself.

Who am I kidding? We all know I'll probably get a kiddie-size frozen yogurt and pretend it's the same.

I'm good at pretending. Like right now, as I smile wistfully at Levi. Of course, I'm imagining him as Josh, and feeling all the things I feel knowing that we can't be together.

At least in the show, there's a good reason, like systemic racism and prejudice. In real life, it's a complete and total personal rejection. Still, I do what

I've always done. Stuff my feelings way deep down and plow ahead.

Try to be the best.

Man, I really do need to get some help. As soon as this show is up and running, I'm going to contact Gloria's therapist. I can't continue on this way.

On the other hand, if I didn't have this foolish drive to be the best—to do my best—there's no way this show would come together. The Edison needs my drive right now. We've finished our first dress rehearsal and the rest of the cast has dispersed. We're down to the last twenty-four hours before the show, and I still need to work on my stuff. So work away I will.

Plus, when I'm pushing myself on the lyra and the silks, I don't have room to think about Josh. Upside down and spinning, I'm not thinking about that adorable eyebrow thing he does while he's playing the piano and conducting all at the same time. It's like he's giving you this secret message with them.

I also don't have to think about his variety of smiles, including the wide smile, the half-grin, and my personal favorite, the lower lip bite.

Nope, not thinking about that one at all.

Even though it's evening, it's hot and humid and the sweat pours off me. I wipe my hands on my leggings and try again. I know I'm on the lyra the right way when my bruised spots are bearing all my weight. It doesn't matter.

The only thing worse than thinking about Josh is thinking about what parts of my body hurt. I'm not sure that there's anything that isn't screaming at me right now. I flip down off the lyra to get a drink of water.

I'm sweating so much that I haven't had to use the bathroom, despite the two liters of water I've packed away this afternoon. My phone rings.

"Hey, Mom." I'm out of breath.

"Oh, did I get you at a bad time?"

"Just stopped for a water break. We're in the home stretch now. Tomorrow's opening night. We only have one more run-through tomorrow before it's real."

I wipe the sweat that refuses to stop pouring off of my face. Ugh. I'm totally going to have to wash my hair tonight. I don't have the curliest or coarsest hair out there, but at its length it's still tons of work. It's going to add at least two hours onto my night to dry and straighten it so I can get a wig on my head tomorrow. I try to minimize how often I straighten it because the heat can really damage my hair. But with this amount of volume, they'd never get that pink Gibson girl wig on over it if I left it curly.

I catch Mom up on everything and then get back to work. It's only after I finish my routines for the third time that I realize my critical error. My hands had sweat through all the chalk, and I didn't bother to replace it. Red callouses now line my palms, angry and sore.

I guess I'm done for the night.

By the time I grab a bite to eat, shower, wash and condition my hair, and then comb through it, it's well after midnight. Even though it will be more of a pain,

I decide to go to bed with wet hair and straighten it in the morning.

Seven a.m. me hates the decision that one a.m. me made as I yank the flat iron through my hair. One a.m. me didn't consider that those blisters on my hands would be even angrier and would tear open while gripping the hot tool.

Shit.

I blow on my hands, trying to dissipate the pain. My next move is to go to Amazon and order a pair of trapeze gloves. Yes, such a thing exists. I'll have to tape over my hands today, which means my grips are going to feel weird. I'd better go and practice with the tape.

Still, because I'm a glutton for punishment, I try one time with my bare hands. That's a hard no. My blisters are now angrier, and I need to clean them well so they don't get infected.

I'm so distracted by my hands that I almost don't see Josh in the hall outside the bathroom. *Almost.*

"Hey," he says.

I'm tired, I'm hungry, and I hurt like hell. I'm also scared to death about going on stage tonight. The last thing I need is Josh jerking me around by being nice to me, only to pull away when I lean in. "Nope." I shake my head.

"Nope? What nope?"

"Nope, I'm not doing this today. I can't talk to you."

He puts his hand on my arm to stop me. "Les, what's wrong?"

"You. Everything."

"Me? What have I ever done to you?"

"You won't let me in. You're shutting me out."

"Do you blame me?"

I look at him. His hazel eyes are accusing. "Josh, that was so long ago. We were kids. You've got to move on."

He scuffs his foot on the ground. "Some things are easier said than done."

"So there's no hope for us?"

Josh shakes his head. My heart, holding onto a small bit of hope, breaks into a million little pieces. "I can't, Leslie. And it's not just that I can't; I don't want to."

He turns and walks away.

I stand there numb, kicking myself for saying anything. This is infinitely worse than how I was feeling before. Tears fill my eyes. He's never going to forgive me.

Not thinking, I grab a bottle of alcohol from my bag and take it to the bathroom. I pour it over my hands, trying to wash away any germs that might invade and infect me. You know, like the seeds of hope I'd held in my heart.

The stinging brings tears to my eyes. All I can feel is the burning in my hands. This real, tangible pain, rather than the one expanding in my chest, threatening to consume me whole.

Yes, this terrible pain in my hands is better. I pour alcohol on the other hand, tears flowing freely as I gasp with shock. This burning is so intense, I can focus on nothing else.

I walk out of the bathroom, wincing as I have to use my hand to pull open the door. No one's around, so I don't bother to hide my tears—

"Leslie, are you okay? What's wrong?"

Oh shit. It's Tabitha. I can't let her see me cry. I wipe my eyes with the back of my hand. Well, that was a dumb move. Tabitha sees my jacked-up palm and grabs it. "Seriously, Leslie, are you okay? This looks bad. Should we get someone to look at it? You've really torn up your skin here."

"Yeah, I just poured some alcohol on it to clean it. It brought tears to my eyes." I wave my hands, trying to dry off the alcohol in the hopes that it stops burning. "I'll be fine in a second. I just don't want this to get infected."

Tabitha takes my hand again, examining it. Her eyes are wide and her mouth is open in a shocked "O" shape. "What are we going to do? Do Henderson and Grayson know? Have you told Levi? Can you change the choreography?"

As if. I'm going to push through this, as I do everything else in my life. It's like my hands are a metaphor for me. I shake my head. "I'll be good. I need to air it out for now. I didn't use enough chalk last night and this morning. I'll tape it for tonight. I think I might have the seamstress bedazzle a pair of trapeze gloves to match my costume. I ordered them on Prime, so they should be here by tomorrow."

They didn't have a lot of color choices, so I hope we can do something to hide the black wrist straps. My costume is so gorgeous that I don't want the stupid gloves to detract from the overall look.

Tabitha looks me up and down, still holding onto my hand. She's probably going to call me crazy. "Damn, girl. You are a badass."

That's not what I was expecting to hear. I never expect to hear something good or positive. Only the negative. Probably because that's all I ever tell myself. I don't know how to accept Tabitha's compliment.

I pull my hand from hers. "Yeah, well, the hand is the least of my issues." At least you can see the injuries on my hands and the bruises on my legs. No one can see that my heart is broken. I continue, "I've been a ballerina for years. My feet have seen worse and still performed. I'm not saying it feels awesome, but you know, the show must go on. Is it really a show if someone's not bleeding?"

Tabitha shakes her head. "You're my hero. But when this is all healed, I'm taking you for the most luxurious manicure this town has ever seen. Complete with paraffin and hot towels and a bottle of champagne."

That mental image is enough to make me smile for the first time today. Probably for the first time in several days. It sounds like heaven. "I don't even really know you, but I'm totally going to take you up on that. Can you find a whole-body paraffin tank? By the end of these three weeks, I'm going to need to soak for about three years. This has all been so crazy."

Crazy is right. Here I am, shooting the breeze and making plans for a girls' spa day with Tabitha Stetson. I heard she hooked up with Jonathan Spencer Maxwell once. I wonder if she'll talk about it as we lie there with face masks and cucumbers on our eyes?

"Well, you're a rock star to me. I've gotta run for a final fitting." And with that, she's gone.

Did that really just happen?

My fall from cloud nine is swift as I realize that the only person I want to share this with is the one person who wants nothing to do with me.

Chapter 18: Josh

These have been the fastest three weeks of my life. I can't believe we're almost to the closing for *The Greatest Showman*. After tonight's performance, there's only tomorrow's matinee left. It's been more amazing than anything I could have ever possibly imagined. Having Tabitha in the cast just elevated The Edison into a brand new stratosphere, and I think she's going to take us all with her. The star power radiates off of her like a comet's tail.

"You heard the rumors, right?" Morgan says to me. "Angie Aliberti and Mandy Calhoun are coming to the show tonight." I think she *squees* a little. Morgan is not the type to squee. "There was a call to the box office, but they said not to tell Tabitha."

"Until I see them both, it's just a rumor, not a fact." Regardless, I still want to look my best for the show. I hightail it into town and find the barber who just laughs at my long hair. "Why don't you check out Fifi's for all those beautiful curls you have?" he suggests.

"Whatever, man. You just lost my business." I head next door to the beauty salon. Let's be honest, they're going to have a much better idea of what to do with my hair than good old Chuck with his straight blade and electric clippers. Thirty minutes later, I have less than half the hair I used to. It's still long enough to give me a rock edge, but I don't have to wear it in a ponytail or a bun anymore.

I wonder if anyone will notice.

There is a moment that makes me sad as I look at the tufts of my hair on the ground. My mom *hated* long hair on guys with a passion. In fact, there was a distinct period where I had a buzz cut because she was afraid it was going to grow overnight and get too long.

A few years after she died, I was so pissed at not having parents anymore that I decided to grow my hair out as an act of rebellion. Like I was going to show the Universe or something.

I look in the mirror and know she would be pleased with my trimmed tresses. Actually, she'd ask me if I wanted to take a few more inches off. Still, it's an improvement for me.

It's not like I'm trying to pick up one of Tabitha's friends or anything, but I don't want them thinking I'm a hobo either. That is if they do come to the show.

They totally come to the show.

Okay, maybe Morgan isn't the only one squeeing here. It's not just because they're famous. Tabitha actually said she'd look at my show this week now that she's done.

And Mandy said she'd look at it too. If they're both looking at it, this might be an actual chance for me.

Plus, it's three-fifths of the Sassy Cats. Tabitha told me the other night that they actually sang with Prince one time. That's why her daughter is named Paisley. She also told me that he was super weird and that they weren't allowed to speak to him or make eye contact with him. Still, it feels like I know Prince by association or something.

All I'm hoping for is to be able to quote Mandy or Tabitha with an endorsement like, "This show doesn't suck," or "Josh has talent and you should listen to him."

Obviously, my talent for writing music far exceeds my talent for writing quotes.

The aftershow coffeehouse cabaret is slowly filling up when I see the trio come in. Tabitha hasn't been to one of these yet. Before I can even stop myself, I'm making a beeline for her table. My mind is whirring so much I can't even think of what I'm going to say. Okay, take a deep breath.

"Wow."

Wow. That's what I manage to come up with. I'll see myself out.

Tabitha—God bless Tabitha—swoops in to save me from acting like more of an idiot. "Josh, you remember Mandy. This is Angie. Angie, this is Josh, our super talented musical director. He's even writing his own show. He showed me some of it last week, and it has potential. You should take a look at it."

She remembered. That's what she led with too. I feel the heat rise to my face as my heart pounds in my chest. I bite my lip, trying to keep my composure and not stand there grinning like a fool.

"Thanks. I'm still working on it. It's got a ways to go." Why can't I just say thanks and leave it at that? I need to shut up.

"You're off to a solid start. Keep going and let's see where it ends up," Tabitha encourages. She's probably just saying that, but I'll live on that compliment for years.

"Josh!" Zak calls from the front of the room. He's opening the cabaret with his version of "God, I Hate Shakespeare" from *Something Rotten*. We'll be doing that show in two weeks, right after the run of *Rock of Ages*. Even though we haven't started rehearsals for *Rotten* yet, the cast often likes to tease the upcoming shows.

I turn to go back to the front of the room to take my place at the piano.

Tabitha stops me. "Josh, if there's room …" She motions between the three of them.

Shut the front door.

I nod and try not to jump up and down as I weave my way to the makeshift stage. I see Tabitha exit the room and then return a bit later with some music in her hand. The three of them have their heads bent together, studying it. We're almost through our planned acts. I manage to catch Tabitha's eye, raising my eyebrow in question.

She waves the music back at me and nods.

As they make their way to the front of the room, I introduce the famous trio, like they need any introduction. "Okay, folks, for our last song of the night, we have a very special act. Our very own Tabby Stetson will be singing, along with her fellow Sassy Cats, Mandy Calhoun, and Angie Aliberti. Please give them a warm welcome."

Tabitha hands me the music from *A Chorus Line*. I'm familiar with it, as we did the show a few years ago. Even if we hadn't, I'm blessed with the ability to read music and play it pretty much on the spot.

I hope wherever my parents are, they can see me right now. My throat tightens, thinking about them. Sometimes those feelings of missing them catch me off guard and totally overwhelm me.

Like right now.

Still, I need to pull myself into the present and enjoy this fantastic moment as these three stars sing to my accompaniment. Tabitha said something about this being a once-in-a-lifetime chance.

I agree, and I'm going to enjoy the hell out of every single moment.

I'm still living this high when we head back to the dorms. No one is in the mood to wind down just yet. There's also plenty of alcohol flowing. I don't get to kick back and relax nearly as much as I'd like to.

Tonight though, I'm taking full advantage. Tabby must feel the same way, as she's back in the dorms, Mandy and Angie in tow. Everyone's here, including Henderson and Grayson. I spy Leslie across the room, and before I can help myself, I smile at her.

Her return smile is small and hesitant.

I guess I deserve that.

I even think about going to talk to her, but then Tabitha pulls my attention away. They're talking about staying here, and how Tabby is totally unprepared for an Upstate New York winter.

If I'm asked later, I'll say I was drunk, but really it's the courage caused by the adrenaline from the night that's to blame for my next statement. "Okay, well then, we'll put 'a southern climate' on our list of needs in order for you to work with me on my show."

Tabitha laughs. "Nice try, Josh. I mean, I'm absolutely going to look at it some more, but don't quote me on anything yet." She takes a sip of her wine. "Wait, Carson Reuben's not here, is he? I mean, otherwise, he'll put out a press release in *Backstage Magazine* tomorrow, and it'll be set in stone."

Damn, if only I'd thought to invite that guy.

Hands down, this has been one of the best nights of my life. And for some reason, I get the feeling that it's all just getting started.

Chapter 19: Leslie

He smiled at me.

Okay, I'm pretty sure he's drunk and is smiling at everyone, but at least he didn't glower at me.

I'm not even sure Josh can glower. What I get is usually more of a scowl. But that's not the expression that's on his face tonight.

He looks so happy.

And he should be. The three Sassy Cats have all but adopted him as their own pet. Sure he may have been the guy in the background playing the piano, but he was on stage with this power trio.

I could see them taking him on tour. He'd be wonderful with them. I could even see him collaborating on music. Maybe someday he'll win a Grammy or something, and I'll tell ... whomever I'm with at the time ... that a long time ago that boy used to love me.

I still want him to love me.

But I need to love myself first.

I'm working on that. Monday's my first appointment with Malachi Andrews, Gloria's therapist. I finally had the courage to call him to schedule something. And then I had to work up the courage to call my parents to ask them to loan me some money.

I've decided that with only four weeks until I have to be back here in Hicklam for *An American in Paris* rehearsals, I might as well just stay. Imani's cousin Jade did agree to sublet my share, so at least I don't have to worry about rent.

Just a place to stay for the next month.

And a way to pay for it.

I'm sure I'll figure something out. There's got to be a restaurant here in town or something.

Grayson slides up next to me. "Well, you did it." He raises his beer in salute, and I match with my glass of wine. I'm a lightweight, mostly because I never drink.

Too many calories.

But the calories be damned, I've earned this toast. "Thanks for the chance and your patience. It was pretty touch and go for a while."

"You bit off a lot—I thought more than you could chew. But you pulled it off."

"I'm anything if not too stubborn to know when to quit. You hired me for something, so I was going to deliver."

Grayson cocks his head. "You know we never expected half of the aerial stuff that you did. We hoped maybe you could sit on the hoop or do a split or something." He laughs. "Actually, it was Tabby who suggested you, and she said something like, 'she's a ballerina so she can do bendy stuff.' All we needed was some bendy stuff, but you came out swinging. Literally."

I laugh. "God, why didn't you tell me? My life would have been so much easier. Do you know that everything, right down to the roots of my hair, hurts?"

"But you know the show wouldn't have been so special."

I do know.

Grayson continues. "So thank you. What you did was superhuman and it may be what moves *Showman* onto the next level."

His praise makes me uncomfortable. Probably because I'm so used to setting impossibly high goals and then berating myself when I can't achieve them.

I'm not used to *actually* being successful.

"Okay, then. Well, so is there a set time I have to be out of here on Monday? Can I stay until then? I mean, I guess I can leave right after the show tomorrow afternoon. I just don't really have my next place lined up yet. I'm sure I'll find something." *Dear God, why am I rambling?* I drain the rest of my wine. What are the odds that my plastic cup will magically refill itself?

Grayson shakes his head. "Don't worry about it."

"Worry about what?"

"Leaving. You're coming right back here in a few weeks. And frankly, your work ethic is something special."

"It's not a work ethic. I'm too stupid to know when to stop."

"Trust me, it's a work ethic that not a lot of people possess. And I'm stupid with a lot of things, but I know the value of hard work."

I look around the room. Everyone here busts their asses to make this place the success it is. "I think everybody does."

"That's why they're here. And that's why I want you to stay during this interim."

"Stay?" I can't be hearing this right. "And do what?" As soon as the words are out of my mouth, I wish I could take them back. No one will ever accuse me of being too delicate or polite, that's for sure.

"We can definitely put you into the ensemble for *Rock of Ages* if you feel like busting your ass again and learning a number or two. After that, we have *Something Rotten*. Definitely ensemble for that, and I think you should be dance captain for both *Rotten* and *An American in Paris*. Obviously, there's a stipend for being dance captain."

"I can't tap. Isn't there a lot of tap in *An American in Paris*?" My mom wanted me to stick with tap lessons, but I only got through grade three before I gave up. It wasn't my jam.

Also, why do I have to open my mouth and be so brutally honest? This is a chance to stay here and get paid for it.

"We can figure that out. You in?"

I glance across the room to see Josh, his wide smile laughing. *Hell yes.*

"I think I can make that work. Thanks, Grayson."

He squeezes me on the shoulder and then stands. I stare into my plastic cup at the dredges of chardonnay, amazed at the turn my life just took.

I stand up, unsure of what to do with myself. This is good. Really good. Yet somehow, I'm not doing the internal cartwheels I expected to be doing. Instead, I feel … out of sorts. I walk outside.

Maybe I'm tired and need some air. Maybe it's the wine. I'm not used to drinking. Maybe it's—

"Hey." Josh is there, walking beside me. "Where you going? It's pretty dark out here."

Instantly, I feel better. Also, he cut his hair, and I like it. A lot.

I look around. The grounds are shrouded in blackness. I hadn't even noticed. "I dunno. I wasn't paying attention."

"Hicklam's pretty safe, but still, you shouldn't be wandering out here alone in the dark."

"If I can survive Brooklyn, I'm sure I can survive here."

Josh looks around. "But you're almost never going to get attacked by a bear in Brooklyn. Here?" He raises his eyebrows, glancing around.

"For serious? A bear?" I face him, my hands on my hips.

"Totally. They have them here. Not to mention coyotes and foxes and other things that seem cute but could be rabid."

I consider him for a moment. "Okay, you can stay with me."

He stands a little taller, puffing out his chest. "So you think I can protect you from a bear? That's a nice confidence boost."

I pull my lips tightly together, not wanting to laugh. I'm not successful. There's a chance I'm tipsy. A good chance.

"What?" he asks, not getting the private joke I have in my head. "What's so funny?"

"I wasn't thinking you'd protect me, per se. I was thinking more along the lines that I can definitely outrun you, so if a bear is chasing us, he'll get you first and I can get away." I laugh a little more than I should. It's official. I'm definitely tipsy. Otherwise, I never would have actually said that out loud.

His mouth drops open for a moment, and then he starts to laugh. Standing here in the dark, we're the two teens who became fast friends and faster lovers. None of the drama of the past decade exists. "I doubt that."

When I'm with Josh, I'm the freest Leslie I can be.

Once we start laughing, neither of us can seem to stop. Wetness runs down my cheeks. It's so nice to be crying this way, rather than out of anger or sadness.

"You honestly think you're faster than me?" I gasp. He's a musician. I'm a highly trained endurance athlete. There's no way he's faster.

Josh doubles down. "I know I am. Ready? On your mark, get set, GO!"

I hear those words and I take off into a sprint. Of course, I'm wearing slides, slightly inebriated, and it's the middle of the night. Obviously, I go down like a sack of potatoes. However, I was in front of Josh just enough that I then became a speed bump for him, causing him to somersault over me.

I can hear the thud as Josh lands flat on his back. In a somewhat state of disorientation myself, I crawl over to where he's splayed on the ground.

"Are you dead? Please tell me you're not dead." I start feeling him up and down, trying to find something that might be a limb in order to check his pulse. I manage to palm his face, squeeze his neck, and then trail my hand down a surprisingly firm abdomen ... because apparently my hand has no sense of direction.

Or knowledge of anatomy on where to find a pulse.

His hand shoots up, grabbing my wrist firmly before I can get into too much trouble. With a yank, he pulls me down onto him.

"I'm keeping you on top of me like a shield so the bear has to eat you first."

We dissolve into giggles again, our bodies flush with one another. After a moment, I realize I'm the only one still laughing. I look into Josh's face. If I weren't an inch from it, I probably couldn't see it.

"This reminds me of sneaking around outside at camp." We had more than one rendezvous outside. It was neither glamorous, nor elegant, but we were horny teenagers and desperate to be together.

"Leslie." His voice is gruff. "I—"

"Don't say anything. Don't. Let's just be who we used to be. For a few more minutes." I want to lean in and kiss him more than anything in this world, but I'm too afraid of him rejecting me. Instead, I put my head down on his chest, terrified to move and end this magical moment. I try to slow down my breathing to match his, feeling his chest rise and fall under mine.

His arms snake around me, holding me tight to him for a moment. I close my eyes, inhaling the scent of him. I don't remember the last time I felt this relaxed. I should tell him I like his hair. I should tell him I'm sorry. I should ...

"Leslie." Suddenly he's shaking me. "Leslie, wake up."

"Huh?" I don't know where I am. It's so dark. Where—oh, I'm still on top of Josh and we're still somewhere outside randomly waiting to be eaten by a bear. "I wasn't sleeping."

"The drool and your snoring says otherwise."

Abruptly, I push myself up and begin feeling his shirt. There, indeed, is a small wet spot.

Oh my God.

"Maybe that bear will come and grab me now, and we'll never have to speak of this moment again." I put my forehead back down on Josh's chest. But he's laughing. I push myself up off of him, standing without an ounce of grace. "I'm sorry."

Josh stands up. "It's a T-shirt. It's not the end of the world."

If it had been with anyone else but Josh, I'd probably run away and never speak to them again. Yet with him, I feel as if I can be honest. "I didn't realize how tired I was." We start walking back toward the dorms. "I don't normally fall asleep that quickly. I much prefer to lie there for hours, thinking about all the mistakes I've made, and then having anxiety about what little time I have left to sleep."

It's a great pattern, let me tell you.

"I don't know how you don't just collapse into bed every night. You run yourself ragged."

I shrug. "I don't know any other way to be. It's what my life has always demanded of me. It's what it takes—"

"To be the best," Josh interjects. "I know. But you know, there's more to life than being the best."

All I know is this quest to be the best cost me a relationship with Josh ten years ago. If there's one consolation I can take from not achieving my goals, it'll be the chance to do this over and get this right.

If he'll let me.

Chapter 20: Josh

I'm starting to figure that out," she says deliberately. "I don't know where the bar should be, I guess."

"It's a place called the 'happy medium.' You should try to find it." I can't believe we're talking like this. I can't believe how quickly I made a beeline for her when I saw her walking outside. I can't believe that in that incredibly intimate moment, she fell asleep.

Leslie continues talking. "My parents always put a tremendous amount of pressure on Meri and me, but it wasn't just them, you know? We lived in the suburban midwest. That means the majority of our peers looked a lot more like my mom than my dad. It also meant that I felt like I had a lot more to prove because I looked more like my dad."

"I'm sure this was tough." I don't know what else to say.

"You know, it was never something I thought about myself. I was just me. Mom is Mom and Dad is

Dad. They're from different cultures, but it's not like I know anything different. What about your parents? Are they from similar backgrounds?"

The moment she mentions my parents—using present tense—it's like the world stops. Usually I know a conversation is going in this direction and I can mentally prepare. I thought we were going to get into a deep discussion about race. Instead, I'm now blindsided by all the feelings I don't want to have.

Even after all these years, the anger is still raw. The injustice of it all. The fact that I can't call my dad to tell him that I finally finished my show, and that people are actually interested in hearing some of it. Or that I can't call my mom to tell her that I was hanging out with the Sassy Cats. She loved them. I can still see her, driving me around in her Honda Odyssey, dancing behind the wheel to "Here Kitty Kitty."

It's not fair.

But Leslie doesn't know this. Of course, she doesn't, because how would she?

And then, my anger goes directly to her.

She should know.

"I don't want to talk about it," I say gruffly. If I say anything else, I'm bound to explode. Quickening my pace, I pull ahead of her.

"Wait, Josh!" she calls. I keep walking. I bound up the stairs, two at a time in an effort to beat a hasty retreat to my room. Once behind the closed door, I ball my hands into fists and press them into my eyes.

Every so often the grief overcomes me. This is one of those moments.

Flopping on my bed, I pick up my phone to text my sister. Kim's probably the only one who can relate.

She doesn't reply. I can't expect her to. It's after two a.m. I'm sure she's sleeping. She's got a baby, so it's not like she's out all night.

I jump when my phone pings. It's a hug emoji.

I hug the phone tightly to my chest, wishing I could hug my mom one more time.

In the morning, I wake up still clutching my phone. The ache is still there, but the rage is gone. At least for now. I'm afraid it'll come back when I see Leslie again.

I need to tell her.

We've got one more show to get through this afternoon, and then Leslie's gone for a bit. She'll be back to work on *An American in Paris*, but I won't have to spend the kind of time with her that I did on this project.

That's good because if I don't have to be around her, I don't actually have to tell her.

I hate telling people about my parents. The looks of pity make me want to punch something, and I'm totally not a violent guy. But also, it makes me relive it every single time.

Once was enough, thank you very much.

I wait until the last possible minute to go in and grab breakfast. Of course, the dining room is still full. The cast is sluggish, and I see more than one person who looks as if they are nursing a hangover.

Hangover.

I think Leslie was a bit drunk herself last night, from the way she tripped, to how she fell asleep on me. Maybe she won't even remember any of it. Then I won't have to tell her. We won't have to talk about those moments lying on the ground and how I wanted to kiss her.

Damn, I'm glad I didn't.

Even if she remembers, I only have to deal with her today before she leaves for a month. I'm sure she will forget me in that time. It only took her a day the last time, and we were much closer then.

All I need is a cup of coffee and then I'll slink over to the rehearsal room.

"Hey." Her voice is soft behind me. I close my eyes for a second, trying to will my face into a neutral expression. "You okay? Things got weird last night."

I turn to face Leslie, trying not to spill my hot coffee. "Sure. Fine. Gotta run. I'm late."

I step past her, ready to let out the breath I didn't know I've been holding. Her hand lands on my arm. "Josh, what happened? I thought ..." She looks down at the floor.

I should tell her, but it's better this way. Let the old embers die down again, smothering the flame out. Otherwise, we're both going to get burned.

I sip my coffee as I walk to the music room. I have plenty of time before I have to start warming up for our last performance of *The Greatest Showman*. We've already been in rehearsals for *Rock of Ages*, and tomorrow the band will hit the ground running with the full score. I sit down at my piano and tinker on the keys with my right hand. Setting my coffee down, I begin playing with both hands, going from one song in the soundtrack to another until I find myself playing "Purple Dawn," the ballad from my own show.

"That's great. You're so talented," Leslie says quietly.

I shrug and run my hand through my hair. It feels so weird now that it's short. Well, shorter than it was. It still wouldn't pass Catholic school dress code, that's for sure.

"That's from the show I'm working on. I wonder if Tabitha really will listen to it." I continue playing the music I've dedicated years of my life to writing.

"What's the show about?" Leslie's standing hesitantly on the other side of the room. While continuing to play, I jerk my head to indicate she should come a little closer. She takes this as an invitation to sit down on the piano bench with me.

I let out a breath and continue playing. I'm usually willing to talk about this show to anyone, at any time. However, when I tell her, it's going to expose me raw. I keep playing, going from one melody to another.

"Josh, talk to me," she pleads.

I take in a deep breath. "It's a contemporary, gender-flipped retelling of Oscar Wilde's *The Importance of Being Earnest*. The title is *Honor Code*, as the heroine's two identities are Dawn and Honor."

Leslie laughs. "Oh God, remember I had to read that stupid play over the summer? I never would have gotten through it without you."

I give her a bland look, my fingers still gliding over the keys.

"Oh," she says. "*Oh*."

I turn away, bowing my head as she makes the connection.

"Josh, is this show for *me*?"

I shake my head. "Not *for* you. Because of you."

Instead of questioning me further, she rests her head on my shoulder, as if we're still in love. "Josh, I'm so happy to be here with you. And I don't say that lightly. I'm not often acquainted with happiness, but when I am, you're the common denominator."

She's leaving tomorrow. I can let her go on this note. I can be the bigger person, and not stomp all over her perceptions. She's got a lot of issues, and I don't need to contribute to them. I can pretend for one more day.

"I think you need to find happiness within yourself, and not try to depend on someone—or something—else to provide it for you. But I'm glad this was a good experience for you. It bodes well for when you come back in a few weeks."

Her head pops up.

I wish she'd put it back.

"Oh! Great news! Grayson asked me to stay. He's adding me to the ensemble. I can even join *Rock of Ages*, but I think I might sit this one out. And he's asked me to dance captain for the next two shows."

My face falls, and there's nothing I can do to hide it. "So, you're staying?"

Her face mirrors mine.

Shit.

"I mean, this is a surprise. I thought the cast was all set. They've already been rehearsing for a week now."

Leslie looks down at her hands. "Do you want me to go?"

Yes. *No.*

"It's not my decision to make. You have to do what's right for you."

She rotates herself so she's facing me. I'm relieved at the distance, feeling like I can finally take a breath. "I'm not sure how many more times I have to tell you I'm sorry. This is the last one. I was a kid, and a super messed up one at that. I'm still messed up, but at least I'm aware of it. I'm even starting therapy tomorrow. I made a mistake, cutting you out like that. It wasn't because I wanted to. It was the only way I knew how to function."

"I don't understand how you could walk away and never look back. How you could claim to love me and then hurt me."

She's holding my gaze for once. "I wasn't in a place to love. I was hurting too much myself."

"You? Hurting?" What did she have to hurt about? She still has her parents.

"Of course I was hurting. My whole life was pain. I hated myself. Only when I was with you did I feel worthy of love. But that kind of love needs to start from within. Without you, I didn't have the spark. I forgot how to feel it. After we left camp, all I did was hurt. So I threw my pain into dance. But it's never gone away. It's always there. And the longer I wasn't a success at ballet, the less worthy I even felt of your love. Of anyone's love. Why would you love someone who was not the best?"

I stare at her for a moment before shifting my gaze down to my hands, still poised over the ivory keys. *I should tell her*. "You weren't the only one who had shit to deal with, you know."

"I know. Teenage shit is rough for all of us. Some people handle it better than others. I apparently don't handle anything well."

Okay, this is it. I'm going to tell her why my emotions seem way out of proportion for a dumb summer fling. "Leslie, it's that—"

"Oh, Josh, there you are. I need a minute, mate." Henderson strides in as if he hasn't just interrupted something important.

Leslie stands up. "Okay, well, I gotta go get ready anyway. See you later." She gives us both a little wave and then walks out, her head hanging.

Henderson's practically reverberating with excitement, which is a bit unusual for him. He's the strong, silent, grumpy type. I've seen him roll his eyes more than I've seen him smile. "So I was looking through your stuff last night. Give me the elevator pitch."

This is it. It's what I've been waiting for. I inhale deeply, ready to deliver in one breath. "It's a gender-flipped contemporary retelling of Oscar Wilde's *The Importance of Being Earnest* called *Honor Code*." And exhale.

"I never read it. Give me a little more."

"A well-to-do woman lives a double life. She's Dawn by birth but goes out and about on the social scene as Honor. Honor is mostly seen through social media. It's a comedy of errors as Dawn/Honor's best friend tries to claim the Honor persona, and they both vie for the attention of the billionaire, George."

Henderson stares off, fixing his gaze on the ceiling. I don't know why he always does this. "What are you thinking for the social media stuff?"

"Acting out the club scenes. Using a projector to show what George sees on his phone."

Henderson nods. "Cast size?"

Mentally, I run through it. "Small. Dawn is the lead. George. The best friend and her love interest. About five or six smaller supporting characters."

"Ensemble?"

Why is he asking for so many details? I'm trying not to get my hopes up here, but I don't think he's asking all these questions to make pleasant conversation.

"I'd like one, but it can be done without. There's a lot still up in the air and open for negotiation." I'm cool. This is cool. I can be cool.

I'm sweating bullets.

Henderson nods, deep in thought. "Okay. Okay. Sounds good, mate."

Sounds good, mate? What's that supposed to mean?

I need to play it suave, though everything inside me is jumping up and down and screaming. Could Henderson be interested in my show? For real? It's one thing for him to listen politely as I ramble on and on about it. It's another thing entirely for him to come to me with a list of specific questions.

"Anything else I can help you with?"

"I'll be in touch if I need anything else." Henderson starts to walk away.

Play it cool. Play it cool.

"Henderson, why the questions? Are you thinking about producing the show? That'd be awesome if you did. I really want you to. What else do you need from me? I'll literally do anything for you to make that happen."

Cool as ice.

"I can't get into details, mostly because I don't have them yet, but I'm trying to run some numbers."

Numbers. People only run numbers when they're trying to figure out if they can make something work.

Holy shit. Henderson's going to produce my show!

Chapter 21: Leslie

Tell me a little bit about why you're here." Malachi Andrews is not what I expected from a psychotherapist.

First off, I automatically pictured an old white dude with wire-rimmed glasses and an ugly checked jacket. Malachi is darker-skinned than me. I'd guess both of his parents are black or brown. It's impossible to tell his age. He could be anywhere from thirty to fifty. He's also bald, and is wearing a soft button-down shirt that probably has some amount of silk in it.

"Gloria told me you helped her." I'm only paying for the time. Why would I start right off with talking about my own needs?

"We're not here to talk about Gloria, so tell me about yourself."

Ah, he sees through my bullshit. I don't know if this is a good thing or a bad thing. "I'm a ballerina. *Was* a ballerina. I tried to be a ballerina."

Jesus, I'm a mess. But that's a given. Otherwise, I wouldn't be here.

"Let's talk about ballet since you started with it."

It's hard for me to remember a time in my life when ballet wasn't a part of it. This is the longest I've gone without attending any sort of ballet class since I was a very young child. "I don't know who I am without it. But now, I don't have it."

"Why did you quit?"

Quit is not even a word in my vocabulary. "I didn't quit. I would never quit. You don't get to be the best by quitting." I look down at my hands, tightly intertwined in my lap. "But no matter what I did, I couldn't be the best. And they saw that. They saw I wasn't good enough. They saw the real me."

"The you who's not good enough?"

I nod. "It's not like I don't try. I try harder than anyone I've ever met. But I always end up just shy of where I need to be. Like, I'm good. Just not good enough."

"And how does that make you feel?"

I don't like how it makes me feel. "Terrible. I hate myself because of it."

"Because you can't be the best? There's only ever one best. That's a pretty high standard to hold yourself to."

"You don't understand. That's what it takes to be in my family. We're literally champions. My father and his father before him. Both played rugby sevens for the Fiji National team. My grandfather was part of the team that won the Hong Kong Sevens in 1976 and 1977, while my dad pitched his way to the Rugby World Cup Sevens championship in 1997. Had Rugby Sevens been in the Olympics back then, they both would have been on the team. By the way, did you know that Fiji won the first-ever Olympic gold medal in 2016, and again in 2021?" I sit up a little taller, filled with pride in my grandfather's home country. That pride is intractably intertwined with my need to be the best.

"That's an impressive pedigree. It's a lot to live up to. Do you play rugby?"

I shrug. "I mean, I technically know *how* to play. Like I know how to drive a stick shift. But like, not enough to actually do it in real life."

"Why ballet instead of rugby?"

I shrug.

"Did you feel like you should be playing rugby?"

His question stops me cold. "I ... I never thought about it."

Malachi lifts an eyebrow. "Interesting, considering you've told me more about Fijian rugby than you have about ballet, and ballet is supposed to be your life."

I thought therapists were supposed to remain impartial and unemotional. That eyebrow was not impartial.

I open my mouth and close it again, trying to come up with an answer. "I never thought about it." I'm repeating myself, but have nothing else to say.

"Interesting."

"Wait, why is that interesting? You barely know me. How can you be making judgments already?"

"I'm not making judgments. I'm trying to get to the bottom of what drives you, and what is causing your maladaptive behavior."

This statement has me on my feet. "Maladaptive behavior? You don't even know me!" There's a good chance I'm yelling a bit.

"Leslie, it's okay, really. I know you have maladaptive behavior because you're here. People don't come to see me unless something's getting in the way."

He may have a point. Slowly, I sink back into my seat. "Yeah, but rugby has nothing to do with it. Ballet is the problem."

"Do you think that maybe, on some level, you're internalizing the feelings of inadequacy that stem not from ballet, but from not fulfilling your family legacy to be an all-star rugby player?"

I mull this over for a moment. "Like I'm a self-fulfilling prophecy of failure because by not playing rugby, I've already failed, so I don't let myself succeed at anything else?"

Malachi raises that eyebrow again.

Dammit. He may be onto something. "But I didn't sabotage myself. I leave it all out there, every single time. No matter what it costs me. I give it my all."

"I saw you in the show last weekend. You were very impressive."

"Thanks. The aerial stuff was new. They called me in because Jasmine got hurt. I'm sure she would have done it better."

"Right. She's the expert. Better than you. So you're not the best. How does that make you feel?"

I ponder that for a moment. I can honestly say I gave it my all. "Surprisingly good. I can only do my best. And considering that I'd never done any of the aerial stuff before I came here, I did pretty damn good." The statement sort of shocks me. I've never been that blasé about it. I add in a little shoulder shrug to show how okay I am with it.

And I truly am.

"Can you ever imagine feeling this way about ballet?"

That's an easy answer. I shake my head. "No."

"May I offer you something to consider?" Casually, Malachi crosses his ankle over his knee, leaning back in his leather swivel chair.

My stomach clenches. I'm not sure I'm ready to hear it. On the other hand, here I am, sitting in a therapist's office. I may not be ready, but it's time. I nod.

"Ballet is impossible for you to win at because you failed by picking it. Whether it's really what your father thinks, or just what you are projecting, you feel that you will always be a failure because you didn't follow in the family's footsteps."

It's the most ridiculous—yet most plausible—thing I've ever heard. "So no matter how good I could be ..."

"You'd never be satisfied. You were dancing at an elite level. A level that most dancers never get to. Given your age," he looks down at the papers on his desk, "I would say that you must have been good to have been with a company as long as you were."

"But I never fully made it to the company. I mean, they called me up when there were several dancers injured, but they didn't renew my contract."

"It sounds to me like they called you up."

"Because of injuries." I fold my arms across my chest. It's an important distinction that he needs to understand. Otherwise, I don't see how he'll be able to help me.

"I'm sure there were other people they could have used. They didn't need you. Were there other ballerinas in the school? You weren't the only one."

"No, they used six of us."

"How many didn't they use?"

Mentally, I run through the class roster, counting off on my fingers. "Twelve."

Malachi tilts his head to the side.

"Fine. I see your point." I don't know if I do, but I'm not telling him that.

"Think about that until next time. Also, the other thing I want you to consider is *why* did you dance? It obviously caused a lot of distress for you. You did it for some reason, though. What is that reason?"

I walk out of Malachi's house after an hour, more confused than ever. I guess I thought he'd tell me what I'm doing wrong and how to fix it.

Once back up at The Edison, I find Gloria, knee-deep in campers learning the opening song to *Newsies*.

"Hey, what're you doing right now? Wanna help?" Gloria nods to the herd of kids. "We could use some help breaking down the dance steps into smaller groups."

"Sure. Show me what to do, and then I'll take a group."

About an hour later, we're putting the smaller groups back together for a run-through. Surprisingly, "Carrying the Banner" is shaping up quickly.

"I'm so glad you stopped in. You're a lifesaver!" Gloria says. "What are you doing this afternoon? I sure could use you for … everything."

"I think I should totally take the music lessons. It's my forte," I kid.

"You weren't bad at all. But, if you don't mind, I'm gonna put you on dance. You're really good at breaking it down. I like how you say it so the kids can remember it."

My very first dance school, the class I was with for years, was a boatload of fun. Often, to remember different steps, we'd call out what the moves resembled. For instance, when we had to pas de chat, someone would say, "oh, the floor is burning my feet" as we hopped from one foot to the other. I employed the same methods today to help the kids—especially those who are not natural dancers—remember the steps.

"I'm open all week, except for my sessions with Malachi. Oh, by the way, did you know that he doesn't just fix everything for you?"

Gloria laughs. "Um, yeah. I've been in more therapy than I can even count. It's all on you."

"But I want him to just fix me."

"He didn't break you. It's not his job to fix you."

I think about it. She's right. "You know, I'm not sure I'm broken. Definitely bent. But if I was broken, I couldn't be fixed. And that's not an outcome I am willing to accept."

Gloria smiles. "Attagirl. Now, let's get back to work. These paperboys aren't going to form a union all by themselves."

And just like that, I'm in another role here at The Edison. Will wonders never cease?

Chapter 22: Josh

So, Josh, we have something we'd like to discuss with you." Grayson motions for me to sit down in his office.

Oh God, here it comes. The moment I've been waiting for. I may throw up. *Stay cool. Stay cool. Stay cool.* Sweat pools in my armpits and trickles down my back. My stomach turns over, and not in a good way.

"Oh my God, is it what I think it is? Are you really thinking about doing it? I can't believe you're thinking about it." I can't believe how many times I used the word "think." I also can't believe how incredibly *not cool* that was.

Grayson smiles. "Henderson and Tabitha would like to produce your show. Here, at The Edison."

Tabitha is in on it too? This is bigger than I thought. I'm definitely going to throw up.

"Okay," I say, my voice high and strained. So much for staying cool. I sound like a twelve-year-old going through puberty.

"We're thinking of something new. Henderson would like to expand The Edison's season, and we're thinking maybe the beginning of November."

The feeling of excitement turns to full-on nausea as doubt and panic take over. *Honor Code* isn't finished yet. I've written the music, but still have yet to do the full orchestration. The script needs work. I'd planned to get someone to take a look at it and help me with it. There's no choreography to it, and I'm not even sure the songs are any good.

"Sure," I squeak out. "Totally. November. That's a super reasonable timeline."

Grayson breaks into his trademark grin. "Dude, you're sweating bullets. You know and I know November is out of the question."

"You didn't say *which* November." I cover quickly.

He laughs. "Good point. In reality, we're thinking March. Get through the worst of the winter weather before we are scheduled to open."

It's the beginning of July. March, a mere eight months away, *might* be doable. That is, if I don't eat, sleep, or breathe anything but *Honor Code*. No biggie. It's only the defining moment of my career.

Grayson continues. "We'd be looking to rehearse for about a month before we open. A little bit of a slower pace than during the season, but the rehearsal schedule may not be as intense."

"A month sounds good," I mumble. I don't know what else to say. My mind is swirling with about a thousand thoughts all at once. "Tabitha Stetson? The Tabby Cat?"

Of course, this is what pops out.

Grayson smiles. "Tabitha has graciously offered to be your executive producer, which basically means she's bankrolling the whole show. The Edison is contributing some. Henderson was ready to pound the pavement trying to fundraise, but he won't need to sell his body on the street corner, thanks to Tabitha."

I sit there for a moment, still trying to make heads or tails of this.

"We're going to offer you three thousand for performance rights. I know this is below what The Edison usually budgets for this, but I think, based on the circumstances, you'll agree it is fair and reasonable." He hastily adds, "This is in addition to the salary for director. If you want to do the music as well, we'll factor that in. Otherwise, let me know who you want for the musical direction."

I sit there, stunned. It's like my birthday, Christmas, and Halloween, all rolled into one.

"So," Grayson keeps going, since I've apparently lost the ability to speak. "We need you to button this down. I didn't see orchestration in here. Are you hiring someone to do it, or will you be taking care of it?"

I'd always envisioned writing all the parts myself, but based on the accelerated timeline, I may need to call in reinforcements. "I'll work on it with some buddies. I'll have that done by November."

Grayson cocks his eyebrow.

"Right. December, January at the latest." I'll have to see if Don and Jen will work on it with me. Maybe D'von can do the percussion. Teamwork will make this dream work.

I walk out of the office, floating on air. My first thought is that I need to call my parents.

Shit.

It's been ten years, and I still pick up the phone to call them. Instead, I call Kim. "Clear your calendar for March. You're coming to see my show at The Edison."

My sister is used to my energy. "What's the show? Are you doing *Hamilton*? I love that music. You should totally do *Hamilton*."

I shake my head. "No, Kim. My show. Like *my show*."

There's silence on the line. I take that as my cue to continue.

"And the best part is that Tabitha Stetson from the Sassy Cats is the producer. She's funding it. Probably going to be in it as well. Like, I'm going to be working closely with her."

"Oh my God."

"Right? It's happening, Kim. It's actually happening." Out of the corner of my eye, I catch some movement. I turn to see who else is out in the garden with me. I don't see anyone.

"Joshy, this is so good. I'd say I can't believe it, but I can. You're so talented and such a hard worker. I knew it would pay off. Thanks for calling me. I needed this good news today." Her voice drops, betraying her sadness.

"What's wrong?"

"Oh, you know. The usual."

"Kim, why don't you move down here? It would be better to see you more often. A change of scenery wouldn't be the worst thing." I worry about her, up in New Hampshire, all by herself.

"No, I'll be fine. I'm glad you called."

"Me too. I love you, you know."

I hear my sister sniffle. Great. I've gone and made her cry. I try never to do that, but it seems like she's crying more than she's not these days.

"I love you too, Joshy-poo. Keep me posted about your hanging with the famous people. Just don't get so famous that you forget your big sister."

"I'll never forget you. Ever. I love you too much to forget you."

After I hang up, I turn to see Leslie standing there. I *knew* I heard someone out here with me.

"Was that your girlfriend?"

"No. I don't have a girlfriend." I frown, wondering why she was eavesdropping on me.

"What about the girl from the car?"

The girl from the car? Then I remember the conversation with Mei. "Oh, yeah, no. We're done. Mostly because she's screwing our bass player. But she didn't really matter to me."

"Not like the girl on the phone. The one that you love."

"Why do you care?"

Leslie stops scuffing the rocks on the grounds to give me an exasperated look. "Come on, Josh. You can't be that obtuse."

"It was my sister. I had some great news and had to share. Kim's my go-to when I have news. She's always the first one I tell."

"That's nice. I don't really talk to my sister. She hates me, but I don't know why. My parents tell me it's in my head." Leslie looks up at me, tapping the side of her head. "I know there's a lot up there that's not right, but I'm not imagining that Meredith hates me."

"I can't imagine life without my sister. I don't know how I would have gotten through everything if we didn't have each other."

Leslie's eyes fill up. "That's how I always thought it should be with Meri and me. Like, we're sisters. But she doesn't have any patience for me. Never has. I think she's still pissed at me for being born and taking away her only child status. And my parents are tired of refereeing, so they just take her side. I feel as if it's another way I've let them down. Your parents must be so happy that you and your sister are close."

I suck in a deep breath and start talking before I have too much time to think. "I imagine if my parents were here, they'd be pleased. On the other hand, I'm not sure Kim and I would have the same relationship if my parents were still alive."

Leslie's eyes go wide as her mouth drops open. Quickly, her hand covers her lower face. "Oh my God, Josh, what happened? When?"

I run my fingers through my hair, still not used to the new shorter length. I don't want to have this conversation, but I know I can't avoid it any longer. "They were killed by a drunk driver." Maybe I can leave it at that and not have to tell her the rest.

"When? How? Oh my God, I'm so sorry." Leslie reaches out and lays her hand gently on my arm.

I look away, biting my lip as the pain is as real as it was that Sunday morning. "It's been almost ten years, but it still feels like yesterday. In fact, before I called Kim, I had the urge to call my mom. And then it hit me all over again."

"Ten years ago? Like when we were at camp?"

I kick the dirt as if it will dissipate some of my anger. "The day after. I slept in, too tired to go to church with them. I'd been up most of the night, trying to figure out why I couldn't connect with you on social media. On their way home from church, some asshole with a blood-alcohol level three times the legal limit plowed into them, going the wrong way on the highway."

Tears fill my eyes. I can usually tell the story without crying, but this is different. All I can feel is the hurt and betrayal I felt that morning before my world ended.

"Josh." She tries to hug me, but I pull away, shrugging her off.

"Don't. You weren't there for me then. You don't get to be here for me now." Childish for sure, but no one ever accused anger of being rational. And try as I might, I still can't separate the anger and pain of losing the most important things in my life in a span of two days. There's a rational part of me that *knows* Leslie's reasons, but I can't separate it from the deep-seated pain I felt as a teenager.

"I ... I didn't know."

"No, because you'd already ghosted me." I turn to face her. "Let me ask you this—if you'd known, what would you have done?"

Her mouth opens and closes, trying unsuccessfully to form words.

"I'm guessing you wouldn't have done anything differently. It wasn't like you had anything to give me," I hiss. I needed something. Anything. And she couldn't. Wouldn't.

Leslie reaches up hesitantly and touches my cheek. "No, I wouldn't have been able to do anything differently. I wasn't in the right place. In fact, I was in a very wrong place. But that doesn't mean that I can't be sorry for your loss. And sorry that I wasn't the person you needed."

"I did need you. And I was so angry with you for a long time. You know, my last few conversations with my mom were about you. And I hated that. I hate that. I should have told her about the stuff I learned at camp. I should have thanked her for teaching me about music. I should have told her I loved her. Instead, I was whining about how I thought you were blowing me off. Mom, God love her, told me I was overreacting. That she never could imagine someone not wanting to talk to me." This is a huge part of what's bothering me, that I wasted my last conversation with my mom on someone who didn't matter. I whisper, "I should have told her I loved her."

Emotions take over, preventing coherent thoughts. All I have in this moment are feelings. Big feelings. Crushing feelings. Feelings I've been trying to ignore for way too long. But now that I've said it out loud, it's like a weight begins to float off of my chest.

Now Leslie is holding my face in both her hands. I want to look away, but I can't. "Josh, she knows you love her. And she knows you love music. And I'm so, so sorry for … everything."

I look into her eyes. They're dark with her emotion—sorrow, regret, caring, empathy. She knows she messed up. But in reality, we were both in a dark place in our lives. It's hard to hold a grudge when you know someone was struggling as much as you were. It's time to let go.

I lean in and kiss her.

It's tentative at first. Of course, I'm cautious. I have every reason to be. But the moment my lips make contact with hers, caution goes out the window. It's replaced by a hunger that has been denied for years. Her body melts into mine. It's as if our mouths have been starved for each other. As our mouths stay connected, all the anger drains out of me, passion and need taking its place.

I'm not sure I'll ever be able to stop.

Chapter 23: Leslie

There are entirely too many emotions running through my brain. Sorrow. Regret. Want. Need. Lust.

Those last three are pretty much in the driver's seat. I was already holding Josh's face in my hands. I press my body into his, deepening our kiss.

I've wanted to do this since the moment I saw him at the train station. Hell, I was thinking about it since the moment I saw his name on the website. But up until his mouth landed on mine, he had not been on the same page. Wait, why is he now? And how can he be after what he just revealed to me?

What a horrible, horrible thing to have happened. Not to mention that I'd destroyed him the day before.

No wonder he hates me. But this kiss doesn't feel like hate.

I pull back, panting slightly. "Josh, wait. Stop for a second."

His hazel eyes search mine. He's out of breath too. "No. I mean okay. Why?"

"That's what I wanted to ask you. Why? Why now? You've been so angry and distant. And you have a right to be." My heart squeezes, the pain palpable, thinking about what he went through then—and since. "Every time we start to get close, you pull back. So what's changed?"

I'm still the person who ghosted you when you needed me the most.

His hands drop, and even though there are only inches between us, I feel like it's miles. "I don't know."

What's that supposed to mean? And what are we doing here? Is he ready to forgive me? Am I ready for this?

I am so not ready for this. I want to be, but I know I'm not. "Josh, I messed this up once before. I don't want to mess it up again. I was careless with your heart. I don't want to be careless anymore, but I'm not sure I know how to be careful just yet."

I don't want to hurt him again. But I'm not ready for this. I mean, my lady bits are screaming that they're *totally* ready. My brain is a different story.

My brain knows I have to slow down if only to avoid hurting Josh—inadvertently—again.

He looks at the ground. "What are we supposed to do then?"

"We can be friends for now. You know, we started off as friends, those first four weeks at camp. We were good that way." I'd rather have him as my friend than have nothing with him. I need to do this right this time. Yes, slow is the way to go.

"Do you think we can really go back?"

I shrug. "I don't know, but we can try, right?" I reach out, threading my hand through his. "I want to be there for you. To prove that I can." To both him and myself, though, the idea of being someone else's support seems quite daunting.

"Friends," he repeats, his tone flat. Then Josh shakes his head.

Oh my God, what am I doing? I don't want to be just friends. I want to be so much more than that.

"No, wait. Forget I said anything. Let's go." I step in, trying to kiss him again.

He puts his hands up to stop me. "I believe in going with your gut instinct. If yours said to put the brakes on this, then we probably should."

"Wait? Do you want to stop?" Now I'm getting all confused.

"No. My gut is currently speaking to me through my more primitive urges. However, my actual brain is telling me that if you have any reservations whatsoever, we shouldn't go any further. I already got burned by you once. I don't need to do it again."

Um, okay.

He's not wrong, but man, that's like a bucket of ice water.

"Will our timing ever be right?" I ask. Of course, what I mean is *will I ever be healthy enough to do this*? I'm not going to phrase it like that though.

Josh laughs tightly. "Right? First it's you and ballet. And now me and ... oh!" It's like a lightbulb goes off in his head. "Oh, man. I've got to go. I've got so much to do. Sorry. Catch you later!"

Then he's gone, jogging off with a purpose.

Okay then.

It's probably a good thing I have another appointment with Malachi in an hour. I'm going to need to work all this out. I should probably look for a part-time job if only to pay for all the therapy I am going to need.

I can think of little besides Josh, and not in a friends-only sort of way. As I plop onto the sofa in Malachi's office, I launch right in. "I need you to fix me so I can have a relationship."

I say this as Malachi's taking a sip of his coffee, which he manages to then spit all over his desk. He apologizes, standing up to wipe off his desk with a tissue.

I'm not nearly as amused. "I didn't realize I was so funny."

"That was not my finest, most professional moment. I'm sorry. It's just not at all what I expected you to lead with today."

"Well, it's what I want to focus on. You already figured out that I'm a self-fulfilling prophecy of failure because I didn't pick rugby. That's one problem solved. Cross it off the list. Now all we have to do is figure out the eating thing, and then I should be good to go for a relationship." I think about the encounter with Josh and how jealous I got when he was on the phone with his sister. Quickly, I add, "Oh, and I should probably have a better relationship with my sister. She hates me."

Malachi has paused with his mug of coffee raised to his mouth. "You done?" he asks. I nod and then he proceeds to take a small sip. "Much better when it's not all over my desk. So, let's talk about the eating thing. But also you know that you are a work in progress, and simply identifying the problem doesn't mean it's solved. But back to food."

I shrug. "It's so clichéd, it's not even funny. Ballerina with an eating disorder. Like, I don't even have to explain it."

"But you do, because eating disorders are intensely personal, and almost never about food, which I'm sure you know. When was the first time you remember consciously restricting?"

Deep down, I do know it was never about the food. And when did it even start? I think back. "It was when I was at the Columbus Academy of Ballet. CAB. I was probably about fourteen. Maybe fifteen. I'd definitely hit puberty because the girls were there." I motion down to my ample chest. "It was bad enough that I already stood out. But I'd gotten my period, which most of my classmates hadn't. And my body changed."

"Did anyone comment about your weight?"

Another shrug. "Probably. But not in a 'you're fat' kind of way. It wasn't one of those ballet schools that encouraged girls to starve themselves so they didn't get their periods or anything." Sadly, those environments exist. "I actually think they were trying to be tactful." The comments float back through my brain as if someone in the room were saying them.

Body composition.
Puberty.
Thick frame.
Heavy muscles.

Stocky.

Developing.

She's got a black body.

"I think the worst one was when they said I had a black body. Up until that point, I really thought they saw me as the same as everyone else. But they were judging me based on the one thing I had no control over—my race."

"If you were fifteen and that was the first time that happened to you, you were probably lucky."

Malachi would know.

I continue, "Well, no, obviously people start forming opinions and making judgments the minute I walk into the room. Do you know what it's like to have to try and get all this hair into a tame bun?"

Malachi's lips form a tight line as the sun reflects off his polished head.

"Oops, sorry. But you know what I mean." I continue, "I'm not sure how old I was when I became aware of the surprised looks on people's faces when I'd show up next to my mom. Or when my dad would walk in, his skin several shades darker than my own. Or my favorite, when I'd meet people in person that I'd only spoken to on the phone, and they told me they were surprised because I didn't 'sound black.' I always wanted to respond that they didn't sound like a moron, but I never had the courage. The black kids at school always called me 'light-skinned,' which made me different from them. My friends—who were mostly white—never even considered me part-white until they saw my mom. Again, I was different. Hell, the only reason I even think about my race is because of the reactions of other people. Man, it's exhausting. Soul crushing. Every single day, it would suck a little part of me away. But in the ballet studio, with our identical black leotards and pink tights, I'd always felt the same. It wasn't until I was a teen that I realized *they* considered me different."

He nods. "And so ..."

The thoughts begin to line up, finally making sense. "I thought that if I could make my body more streamlined, more thin, more *European*, I'd look more like everyone else. That I'd fit in."

"Did you think you were overweight?"

"No, not at all. But I had junk in my trunk. Not to mention the girls here." I gesture to my chest. "I knew if I lost weight those might get smaller. Do you know the irony? Fijian people don't share the same build and bone structure as some of the more well-known Polynesian peoples, like Samoans or Maori. They tend to be lean and streamlined. I get my stock from my mom's hearty Irish peasant and Bavarian heritage. The Germans are known for an ample bosom. But again, people just thought it was because I was black. Or part-black."

"You were trying to control something you had no control over."

"I can control how big my chest gets." Not really, but at my thinnest, I was a cup size smaller. They didn't bounce around as much. It was nice. I mean, I still couldn't wear a leotard without a sports bra like everyone else, but the diminished jiggling was a welcome reprieve.

"You can't control your race. You can't control your bone structure or body composition. You have to accept them."

I don't like that word. "To accept sounds like I'm settling. And when you settle, you aren't doing your best. You don't get to be the best by settling."

"You can't ever be the best if you don't accept who you are and what you bring to the table. And trying to control those things by controlling your food intake is not going to get to the bottom of the actual issue."

"So in trying to solve one problem, I created another?"

Malachi nods.

"And it's not actually about food. It's about who I am. I was trying to change it by not eating."

Malachi nods again.

"Well, that's pretty stupid. If someone explained that to me ten or more years ago, I ..."

"What would you have done?"

In all honesty, I don't know. Probably exactly what I did. Kept pushing forward. "I would have kept trying to change who I was."

"Why?"

"If I knew the answer to that question, I wouldn't be here."

"When you figure out that answer, you'll be able to move forward. You have some homework to do."

"Then I'll be fixed?"

"Fixed implies that you're broken. You're not. You're growing."

I like that mindset—*growing*—better than anything I've ever thought about myself, which is probably why I'm in desperate need of therapy.

It's another one to remember for my merch collection.

I walk back up the hill to The Edison.

When I figure this out, Josh and I don't have to be only friends.

Chapter 24: Josh

The summer is flying by. I need time to slow down so I can get this damn show finished. The orchestrations are taking me a lot longer than I'd planned. The book still needs tons of work, and I'm not even sure all the songs are right.

The only thing I'm sure of is that I'm not sure of any of it.

"Howzit going? Makin' progress, mate?" Henderson slides into the chair next to the piano bench. I'm in my usual posture, hunched over the keys, furiously scribbling notes as I try to figure this out.

"Great. Awesome. Swell. Totally ..." I run out of synonyms. "Rad," I limply finish.

"That bad?" Henderson laughs.

"Not bad, but not as fast as I'd hoped. There aren't enough hours in the day."

"Story of m'life, mate. If there's anything I can do to help, hit me up. You're not doing this alone. It's a team effort, which is code for 'both our arses are on the line.' "

"You sure Tabitha is okay with this? It's a lot of money." I guess I'd sort of had an idea about the cost of one of these things, but until Grayson sat down and laid it all out, I'd been in a happy little world of denial.

It's a lot of money.

"Tabitha says she's all in. But if it'd make you feel better to put together a number or two to show her, have at it."

I exhale. It's not a bad idea, but it'd be a lot of work. We're starting rehearsals for *An American in Paris* tomorrow, having just wrapped *Rock of Ages*. It's the last time for the summer we'll be in double rehearsals. This is the point in the season where burnout starts to set in. I'm not sure anyone in the cast or crew has anything extra to give.

"I'll work on it. Is she staying through for the season?" When we open *Paris*, we won't be rehearsing for another show. "I might be able to teach to some cast something that last week so we have something to perform for Tabitha."

Henderson stands up. "Tabitha's staying on through, so she's got some time. Sounds like a solid plan. I'll let her know. One number, maybe two?" He looks hopeful.

"Sure thing." I should shut my mouth before I commit to anything else. When Henderson leaves, I bang my head on the keys, the disharmony echoing through the music room.

"I don't know much about music, but I'm pretty sure you're not supposed to play the piano with your face."

I don't lift my head when I hear Leslie's voice. Even though it's been almost two weeks since that kiss, I can't stop thinking about it. But we agreed on friends, which is all she can do right now.

It's been easier for me to avoid her than to have to fight my feelings. The irony of that is not lost on me. Plus, I've been super busy. I think she has too. She got pulled right into helping Gloria with the camp and is entrenched with the current production of *Something Rotten*. There's not a lot of time for fraternizing.

I mean, I'm sure I could find the time if I wanted to. Which I do. Which is why I don't find the time.

Not to mention this stupid show.

We haven't made any public announcements yet. We're waiting until the end of the season before making it official. I'm happy for the breather to give me more time to work on it. Once the announcement is made, the pressure is going to ratchet up exponentially.

I should tell Leslie at least. It's something a friend would share with another friend.

Sitting up, I open my mouth to tell her about *Honor Code*. Instead, I ramble, "Are you ready for *Paris*? Kori said she started working with you last week on some of the dance stuff. Do you know which show you'll be doing the lead in? Are your parents coming out to see you? Did you ever talk to your sister?"

Jesus, I sound like an idiot.

"I've been putting off calling Meri. I know I should. I need to talk to Malachi about it before I do it. See if he can tell me what to say."

I didn't think this was how things worked with a psychologist. I went through some counseling after my parents died, but maybe therapy is different? "Is that what he does? Tell you what to do?"

She laughs. "No. In fact, every time I tell him I want him to tell me how to fix things, he laughs. Like actually laughs at me. And then he makes me figure out what the actual issue is, and then I have to actually work on it."

"So what you're saying is that if you put in the effort to figure out the problem from the onset, you wouldn't have to pay him?"

"Yeah, but I feel so much more authentic spending tons of money that I don't have," Leslie laughs. "I could never in a million years get to the bottom of most of my issues without him. He totally steers me in the right direction. Like, did you know that my eating disorder wasn't about food? It was about my attempt to control something because I had no control over my race and how different I was from everyone else."

I try to make sense of what she's saying. "Explain that again?"

"So I couldn't control the fact that I'm biracial. Obviously. It's who I am. But, compared to everyone else in my class in Ohio, I looked black. And then to the black community, I'm light. It's exhausting trying to fit in but never succeeding. And I couldn't control the fact that I hit puberty and developed curves, especially when no one else in class had matured that way yet. I couldn't control the fact that my frame was more muscular and less willowy. What I could control was what I ate. I thought I was doing it to make my body better, but in reality, it was more of a rejection of all those things I perceived as wrong about myself."

That actually does make sense. "So it wasn't because you thought you were fat?"

She shakes her head. "I never did think I was fat. But I was trying to change something about my body that isn't meant to be changed. It would be like trying to change my skin color. It was futile, which is why I never achieved any sort of satisfying resolution."

"And Malachi Andrews helped you figure this out?"

She nods. "Everyone, including myself, just figured it was about thinking I was overweight. I never did, because no matter what I weighed, my body looked the same to me."

I think back to the body that I saw *all* of that summer. It was firm and tight in all the right places and curvy where you would want it to be. "You looked perfect to me. You still do."

She lets out a small gasp and then quickly rearranges her face to cover her surprise.

"I mean as a friend," I quickly cover. "Obviously."

She suppresses a grin. "Obviously, and thank you." Leslie looks at me, her brown eyes luminous. I could totally get lost in them. "But I actually had a point about coming in here. Can you play the pas de deux for me so I can record it? I want to be able to practice it."

"Sure. Got your phone?" I stack up the sheets of music I'd been working on and pull out the score for *An American in Paris*. I nod to her and then start, my fingers flying through Gershwin's trademark melody. Suddenly, I can't wait to see her dance to this.

I wish she'd been cast as the lead. It would let me spend more time with her.

As a friend, naturally.

Once I finish the piece, I say, "I love this music. It's so iconic. It'll be great to see the choreography put to it. Are you and Kori starting with Melinda and Max tomorrow? I think they're arriving tonight."

Leslie tilts her head ever so slightly. "Are those the leads?"

I nod. I flip back to the beginning of my score where I've penciled in the names of the cast. "Melinda Stacy and Max—"

"McGovern," Leslie says flatly. "Of course, it's Max McGovern." She raises her hands in frustration, letting them fall sharply. "For the first time, I'm glad I didn't get cast as Lise."

"I take it you know Max?"

Leslie turns away, crossing her arms over her chest. I stand and put my hands on her shoulders.

"Les, what is it?"

"I know Max. He was with FBBC for a while. I ... uh …. yeah. He's a great dancer though, and will make a good Jerry if he can leave his ego behind."

There's a story there, but I'm not going to push if she's not going to share. I wonder if they were involved? Her reaction was distinct and intense. I wonder what we're in for. Henderson didn't cast Leslie as the lead because he thought she'd bring drama. Perhaps he should have looked a little more closely at his male lead.

"There are a lot of egos here anyway. He'll probably fit right in. Did you get what you need, or do you need me for anything else?" I glance at the pile of sheet music. It hasn't magically orchestrated itself.

Leslie follows my gaze. "What's that?"

"You know, my show." I should tell her the news.

"Still working on it?" She laughs. "Are you ever going to finish it?"

I shrug. "Hopefully someday soon. It's hard with all the other things I have to do, you know?"

Her face falls. "You mean like record music for me?"

I don't want to hurt her, but yes. Exactly. "I'll get it done eventually. The season's wrapping up. *Paris* is the last show. In two weeks, when we're only running one set of rehearsals, I won't know what to do with my free time."

I have no idea why I'm lying to her. All I know is I can't share this with her. Not yet.

Chapter 25: Leslie

Max. Freakin. McGovern.

I walk outside and sit down on one of the garden benches. Why him? Why now? I feel like I'm finally starting to get myself together. He's just going to unravel everything as easily as pulling a string on a sweater.

Subconsciously, I run my hand over my hair, slicked back into a ponytail. Like I need anything else to deal with right now. This was supposed to be the week I tackled calling Meri. Now I have to put that energy into dealing with Max.

I don't want to think about Max. I don't want to think about that time in my life at all. I was a fool, and he's going to remind me of that. I need to do something to take my mind off what's to come.

I head into the dance studio, prepared to start working on the pas de deux combination. Kori gave me the notes and, thanks to Josh, now I have the music. I hook my phone up to the speaker and put some music on to start warming up. My classical warm-up mix isn't cutting it while I do my pliés and tendus, so I hit shuffle. Instead of Tchaikovsky, traditional Polynesian music begins to play.

In order to please my tutu and nau, my father enrolled me in lessons the summers I stayed with them on Oahu. My grandparents couldn't understand why I needed European dance when I had Fijian. Or how I could enjoy a dance that was so controlled and precise when their own native dance was so much more free and spontaneous.

I never did enjoy those lessons. I couldn't seem to let go and tap into that part of myself that wasn't trying to control everything. I was never going to be the best at it, so I didn't see a point in even trying.

But here, in this room by myself, for the first time in my life, I start to let go. The rhythm of the drum beats finally begins to permeate through me as my hips swivel side to side. I try to remember what I was taught all those years ago. I shake my arms and hands out, trying to lose the perfected postures of my ballet training, instead letting the story flow through my hands. I do not only the women's part, but the men's too, as that is much more energetic and fun.

"What is that?" Josh's voice startles me. I stop, slamming my foot down on the floor and pivoting around.

I'm out of breath, sweating, and a large portion of my hair has worked itself free from its tie. I pant as I walk over to the stereo, turning off the music.

"Traditional Polynesian dance. My backup plan was to go get a job as a dancer at a resort," I quip.

"Really? That'd be awesome."

I honestly'd never thought about that until now. It would be something to look into. Tutu and Nau would be pleased at least. "Yes, I'm about to buy my grass skirt and coconut bra." Though, in fact, in Fiji, it's only the men who wear a grass skirt while dancing the meke.

Josh walks over and turns the music back on. He starts the track over and listens, ear tilted toward the speaker, his head nodding slightly to the beat. "This is cool. I like the sound of this. Show me how you dance to it."

Yanking the band free, I shake out my hair and nod for him to start the music. My feet are wide and parallel, something that feels unnatural after so many years of working on my turnout. Toes are flexed, knees bent, arms loose, fingers wide. Polynesian dance is about telling a story through your hands. I try to remember some stories Tutu told me about growing up on the islands.

When the song ends, I sit down on the floor, breathless. My feet are out in front of me, still flexed up, with my knees bent. "So the funny thing is that the word for 'grandfather' in Fijian is tutu. When I first went to ballet class and they talked about getting our tutus for the first time, I was so confused." All I could picture was my grandfather, twirling around on his tiptoes in pink tights and a fluffy skirt. The image still makes me giggle.

"Do you speak Fijian?"

I shake my head. "I know some words. There are certain things we say in our house that we use the Fijian word for rather than English. Like when Dad would yell at the cat, it would always be in Fijian. The cat was a Russian Blue. I don't know why my father thought he'd understand Fijian. But English is the official language in Fiji. Plus, my dad grew up in Hawaii and then California. He wasn't even born in Fiji. He's got more of a Hawaiian surfer dude accent than anything else."

Josh sits down on the floor next to me, his hands tapping out an imaginary rhythm. "That music is cool. I like the beats of it."

I lie down flat on my back and begin stretching, pulling one knee into my chest and then the other. As I extend my leg straight, Josh finally says, "What's the deal with Max?"

I exhale, pulling my shin in close to my nose. Still holding that, I roll over so I'm in a right split. It's one of my favorite things to do.

"We sort of had a fling. Well, not a fling because that would imply that there was like a mutual romantic, emotional connection."

"What was it then?"

I push my hands down into the floor to lift my weight up so I can shift into a straddle split. Then, I rotate again with the left leg in front. "A hookup? The only person Max is interested in is himself. I only wish he'd made that a little more clear before I slept with him."

Mostly because he made me look like a fool. While I was willing to move on and never mention it again, his little comments—always in front of a group of people—made it quite clear that we'd had sex.

He made me feel small and stupid.

"It's fine. He's the type who enjoys the chase and the conquest. He's not deep enough to actually have anything to give another human being." I look down at my hands. I'm not used to opening up this way. Except with Josh. I've always been able to tell Josh everything.

I continue, "It's no big deal, really, but like, he made it very known that we'd slept together. And it made me feel like a fool. Like I'd been stupid enough to fall for his lines and moves. Which, I was, obviously. There's something seductive about someone who's that talented, you know? But the way he said it also sort of implied that I'd slept with him to advance in the company. Like he had that power over me, and I was at his bidding. I don't think he had that kind of pull, but even if he did, that's not why I slept with him. But I didn't want anyone to think that either. Because then, if I did move up, they would think I didn't deserve it."

That I wasn't the best.

"Are you okay with him coming here?" Josh looks genuinely concerned.

"Yeah, I'm a big girl."

He raises his eyebrow at me.

"Seriously, Josh, out of all the mistakes I've made in my life, Max is the least of my concerns. In all honesty, if he wasn't walking through those doors in the morning, he wouldn't even be on my radar." I think back to when I found out Josh was here at The Edison. Yes, Josh definitely took up a lot more mental space than Max McGovern ever will.

"I can talk to him if you want," Josh offers.

I swing both legs in front so they're in the butterfly position. I press the outside of my legs to the ground. "And say what? I slept with her first, so don't be mean?" I bend over, nose to toes.

"Is it even human for you to bend like that?"

Stretching is one of those paradoxical things that hurts but feels so good at the same time. "I'm not even that flexible." I think of some of the ballerinas I've known who were double-jointed everywhere.

"Compared to who? Mrs. Incredible? Good God, I feel my bones dislocating just watching you."

I pat the floor next to me. "Come on and sit. I'll teach you how to stretch."

Josh lowers himself to the floor, barely able to sit cross-legged. I've got my work cut out for me here. I show him a basic hurdler stretch for hamstrings.

There's a lot of grunting and groaning.

"You okay over there?" His face is getting a little red. "Make sure to breathe. Exhale on the hard part of the stretch."

I hear him blow out. "Is this supposed to hurt this much?" he pants, his voice raspy.

"You're going to strain your vocal cords talking like that," I say, taking a page from the voice lessons he gave me oh-so-many years ago.

He lets out a whoosh of air and rolls over to his side. "This is awful. Do you actually enjoy putting your body through this torture?"

I sit up, my back impeccably straight. "Believe it or not, it's worse if I don't stretch. Trust me. So, if stretching is what makes me able to dance, so be it.

It feels less like torture when I put it in that context. Now back to it."

He complies, trying to do the butterfly stretch. I get up and kneel down behind him. Gently, I place my hands on his lower back, guiding his pelvis forward slightly to help with the stretch. My front is inches from his back. As he shifts forward, so do I.

"Do you miss ballet?"

I think for a moment. "I don't miss the environment, which can be toxic at times. But I miss some of the people. And I miss the dance. I'm excited to get into Kori's choreography for this. I'll be happy to lace up my pointe shoes again." Memories of my dance days come flooding back. All that practice. All that work. "Though I have not missed sewing my shoes. That's a huge pain."

"You have to sew your shoes?" Josh sits up a bit, looking over his shoulder at me. His face is only inches from mine.

I wish he would kiss me.

I wish I could kiss him.

I need space.

I sit back, scooting away as if the space will lessen the temptation. "Most people don't know this about pointe shoes. The elastics and ribbons don't come on them, so you have to sew them on every time. And depending on the shoes, there's a lot of customization that can be done too. It can take over an hour for each pair of shoes."

"How many pairs do you need? Like one or two a year?"

This makes me laugh. "Depends on the shoes. For the majority of shoes, they last through about a week of classes. Maybe two or three performances, depending on what you're doing. The principal dancers go through about four pairs a month."

Josh makes a face.

"Yep. The ones I wear last a little longer. I can usually make it about two weeks on one pair. It cuts my sewing in half. And I save more time now that they make them in my color." I pull my bronze Gaynor Mindens out of my bag. "I used to have to color the pink ones with makeup if I was going to be dancing bare-legged. But I've been able to get these since 2017, so it's been another bonus. I mean"—I caress the satin shoe—"there needs to be a bonus for wearing this brand."

"What do you mean?" Josh reaches out and touches my shoe. I hand it to him. He examines it, turning it over. I take the shoe in my hand and tap the floor with it. He follows suit.

"Traditional pointe shoes are made with paper and paste. These have a polycarbonate shank in the middle. Some people consider them 'cheater' shoes because they don't break down like other shoes do."

"Why is the fact that they're durable cheating?"

"Because as the shank breaks down, your foot has to work harder and you get stronger. With the Gaynors, there's the thought that you're not really working. But I like them because they fit my wide foot, and they match my skin. You don't have to break them in the same way. They're about as comfortable as you can get in these torture devices." And as much as I love these shoes, wearing them was *another* way that I was different. Most of the FBBC wore Freeds. There were a few in Blochs. I was the only one with these shoes. No one cared that they were the best for me. They just cared that I was different.

Josh hands the shoe back to me. Pulling tape out of my bag, I wrap my big toes before putting the toe pads on. I slide my foot into my shoe, pointing as I lace the satin ribbons around my ankle. "You know, this is still the thing that makes me feel the best, you know? Like when I'm dancing, I'm finally beautiful."

"You're always beautiful."

My mouth opens slightly, and there's no air left in the room.

And that's okay. I want to exist in a Josh vacuum.

Chapter 26: Josh

In the interest of friendship, I probably shouldn't have said that. On the other hand, watching her dance, uninhibited and free, did *things* to me. Then, when she put her hands on my back to help me stretch, it was all I could do not to flip her over my shoulder and take her right there.

Well, it was easy not to do that because it's not like I'm athletic or coordinated or a caveman. But the *desire* was there.

"Josh," she says, her voice small.

"I don't wanna be friends. I don't wanna do this anymore." I never did. Not from the moment I met her. I always wanted more. Everything else in my life is coming together. Why not take a shot at this?

"Oh." Her mouth closes abruptly. She finishes tying her shoes and stands up, moving to the far end of the studio. I scramble to my feet to chase her.

"No, it's not what you think." I run my hand through my hair, trying to say something—anything— that won't make me sound like an idiot. "You'll never be just a friend to me, Les. You never were. From the first moment I saw you, I was a goner."

She's still facing away. I place my hands on her shoulders and feel her stiffen under my touch. "I know you're not ready, and I'll do my best to be patient, but I can't lie and say what I feel for you is only friendship."

Leslie turns. "I don't want you as a friend either. It seems disrespectful to say it because what I feel for you is so much deeper. But I think we need to take it slow. I'm still a hot mess express, and you've been mad at me for a decade. All that doesn't go away because I want to rip your clothes off and climb you like a tree."

I burst out laughing at her analogy. "You want to *what*?"

She pushes me gently. "Like you haven't been thinking and remembering the sexy times."

I push her hair back behind her ear. Its corkscrew curls are free right now, a change from her normal, constrained style. It's amazing. "Of course I have. It's what's been driving me mad. Do you know how hard it is to stay angry when I'm having all these other *thoughts*?"

She leans in, pressing her abdomen to mine but keeping distance between our faces. "Tell me, Josh, what kind of thoughts?"

I brush her hair back on the other side. My hands remain on either side of her face, cradling her head gently. "I think they require a demonstration rather than an explanation."

I kiss her, our mouths hungry for each other.

This time, there's no holding back.

Well, except for the fact that she's wearing her special dance shoes. I only become aware of this when she rises up on her toes and suddenly is taller than me.

"What the—" I look *up* at her.

Leslie laughs. "Sorry, habit. Let me take these off so we can … you know." She jerks her head toward the door.

With a swiftness of fingers that rivals Jerry Lee Lewis on the keyboard, she's untied her shoes and removed all of the taping and padding that was underneath. I'm not kidding—it was about thirty seconds flat. It was like a pit crew changing tires, only with satin ribbons and weird pouches.

"How did you do that so fast?"

She tosses her shoes in her bag and is on her feet, grabbing my hand. "Never underestimate a dancer's ability to do a quick change. One time, I had ninety seconds to totally change costumes and get my pointe shoes on in between two dances. I did it with ten seconds to spare each night."

I look her up and down, leggings and a cropped T-shirt with a sports bra peeking out. "So if you can get undressed and redressed that quickly, how long until I can get you out of those clothes?"

We're hitting the muggy night air. "We've already established that I can most likely outrun you. I could be naked before you get to your room."

"My room?"

"Unless you want Amy to join us, yes, your room. Wanna race?"

I don't even say anything before taking off in a dead sprint up the hill. We get to the door about the same time, bumping and squeezing as we both try to pass through. I yield an inch, and she squeaks past me.

"What's the big rush? It's not like you can start without me," I tease.

One foot on the stairs, hands on both railings, Leslie looks over her shoulder and raises an eyebrow. "Oh can't I?"

I bite my lip, knowing all the good things she has in store for me. With a speed not many musicians possess, I catch up to her at the top of the stairs, our bodies colliding with each other and then the wall. Leaning in, I grab her wrists, pinning her arms above her head. "Got ya." And then my mouth is on hers again. I trail down, kissing her jaw and her neck before working my way back up to that luscious mouth.

She pushes her body into mine, and I know we'd better get in my room before this becomes indecent. We're lucky no one's seen us yet.

"Come on."

"Oh, I plan on it, and you'd better too."

"Hi."

I wake up to the most gorgeous sound there is. Leslie's voice. She's rolled on her side, looking down at me.

"Hi yourself." I push up onto my elbow, looking over her to see the clock. "What time is it?"

She smiles. "I don't know, and for the first time in my life, I don't care." She flops onto her back.

Oh shit. I spring up. "Leslie, it's 8:47! Rehearsal starts in thirteen minutes. I was supposed to be there at eight!" I glance at my phone, which shows several texts from both Grayson and Henderson. Oops.

"Crap on a cracker!" She's on her feet too. "What are we going to do?"

I'm across the room, pulling a pair of boxer briefs out of my drawer. There's a pair of shorts on the chair, so I grab them too. "Get ready as soon as possible and get down there?" What else would we do?

She stands up, clutching the sheet around her body. Like she needs to, after last night. "But when we both walk in late"—her voice drops—"*people will know.*"

This stops me in my tracks. "Do you not want people to know? What's the problem if they do?"

Her mouth does that adorable opening and closing thing. "We're supposed to be friends."

I step to her, taking her hands. "Lots of people hook up here. No one will think twice. We're consenting adults. It's okay."

She looks at her feet. "It's just ... Max will be here today."

I drop her hands. Right. Max.

"No, it's not like that. I just don't want people to think ... Can you just ..."

I nod, a brick in my gut. Trust. It's going to be harder than I thought with her.

I don't have a fear that she's going to end up back with Max. It's more that I don't think I can trust her to put me first. Above the show. Above ballet. I don't trust that she's not going to ghost me when this is done. We slept together once, and she's already pulling back. It doesn't matter that the chemistry is undeniable. I can't trust her to be there for me. "Fine. I'll see you in rehearsal."

I take about sixty seconds to swipe on deodorant and brush my teeth before running down through the kitchen, snagging a granola bar and a sports drink. Hell, I've done more running in the past nine hours than I have in the past nine years.

I just hope she's worth it.

"Nice of you to join us, mate," Henderson says dryly as I finally make it into the auditorium. "I thought we were meeting here at eight."

"Sorry, overslept." I shove a piece of granola bar in my mouth so I don't say anything stupid.

Grayson looks at the time on his phone. "I don't think we'll have much time to run through things before we get started. Here's the plan for the day. The dancing is the star of this show, so we've got to give Kori ample time."

Some shows are all music and dancing is filler. When you think of *Les Mis*, you don't remember the dance numbers. Conversely, most people don't think of the great songs from *Singing in the Rain*; they think of the dancing. It doesn't mean the other component isn't there, but we have to balance rehearsal time accordingly.

"Kori's going to work with the leads and Leslie, for now, to get that ballet number started. Why don't you work on some of the ensemble pieces?"

I nod, trying not to react when Grayson says her name. Leslie and I obviously need more than thirty seconds to talk this out, but that nagging feeling won't quit.

I didn't get back together with Leslie only to have her blow me off again. I want to trust that she won't.

I hope I can.

Chapter 27: Leslie

I need time. Time to figure out where I am mentally. Time to figure out what happened with Josh last night—and this morning. Time to figure out how I'm going to handle working with Max.

I don't have time for any of it.

I slow my pace to a walk as I enter the auditorium where we're all meeting this morning. I know I'll be in dance rehearsals all day with Kori.

"All right, everyone," Henderson calls, quieting the talking among the cast. "We've almost made it to the end. We're in the home stretch now. One last show to start." He introduces Melinda Stacy and Max McGovern to the rest of us.

It's a struggle not to gag or grimace at his smug, stupid face. I can't believe I let him touch me. I can't suppress the little shiver that goes through me at that thought.

Henderson continues. "Kori's going to get started with Melinda, Max, Braedyn, and Leslie on the dance sequence. That number is about fourteen minutes long. The good news is there's no vocals to learn. The bad news is that it's fourteen minutes of dancing to teach."

There's a murmur through the crowd. I see Max's eyes zero in on me as a sly grin spreads across his face.

Makes me want to take a shower.

Then I notice Josh's gaze darting from me to Max and back again. Great. I do not have time to make heads or tails of any of this. I give Josh a quick, small grin before turning my attention back to Henderson, who's laying out the schedule.

I'm not sure there's enough caffeine to get me through this. Last night was stupid. To be clear, last night was awesome. Staying up most of the night, expending tremendous amounts of energy was stupid.

Henderson dismisses us, and I stand up to follow Kori into the rehearsal room. Max slides up to me, placing a hand on my lower back. "Well, well, well, if it isn't Leslie *Moose*." He emphasizes the last name as if it's an insult.

I twist away from him. "It's Leslie Layne, thank you very much." It still feels weird to say.

"So, you're ... *here*?" he asks.

"Yup. Been here most of the summer." I don't need to tell him how I started or that I'm the understudy. I don't need to give Max any information at all.

"I wondered where you'd slunk off to after FBBC."

"I slunk nowhere. I'm loving my time here at The Edison." I'm not even lying when I say it. If you'd asked me two months ago if I'd ever feel this way, I would have said it would be impossible.

Finding your place in the world does wonders to change your outlook. Also, a good therapist helps tremendously too.

"Have you given up on ballet then?"

Given up. Like a common quitter. No, I tell myself. I did not quit. I moved on with purpose.

Mostly because they forced me out, but potato, pahtato.

We're in the dance room, so I sit down on the floor to put on my ballet shoes. We'll do the warm-up in our soft shoes before going to our pointe shoes. I nod to my feet. "Obviously not. It just looks a little different than before. Why are *you* here?"

He flashes that oh-so-confident grin that makes me want to punch him in the face. "I'm moving to Broadway. I have to pad the resumé first. Make it look like I don't have it too easy."

He's been gunning to fill Robert Fairchild's ballet shoes since I met him.

Kori announces that it's time to start. "Leslie is your dance captain. She'll be leading your barre warm-up today. She's also the alternate for Lise."

Max raises an eyebrow. "Alternate?" he whispers. Except it's the type of whisper your drunk, deaf uncle uses. Everyone turns to look at him.

Kori continues without missing a beat. "Leslie will play Lise in at least two shows, as per her contract. Melinda, I believe you were aware of this?"

She nods. "Grayson called me a few weeks ago." She gives me a small smile. I'll get her on team Leslie, and together we'll defeat the arrogant Max. I smile back.

I pull up my playlist, hooking my phone to the sound system before walking to the middle of the floor. Kori's already moved the portable barre out for me, so I take my place, leading Max, Melinda, and Braedyn in our warm-up. It feels good to call out my favorite combinations from years of technique classes.

It also feels good to know that Max has to listen to me. Male ballet dancers always have a level of prestige due to their scarceness. It's a running joke that females can train from the womb, morning, noon, and night, and still never achieve success. Present company obviously included. But a guy shows interest, anywhere after the age of twelve, and suddenly he's the next Baryshnikov.

Max actually has the talent to back up his swagger. The bedroom prowess, not so much. I giggle at that thought. I see him looking at me, questioning what I find so funny.

I smile sweetly. I'm not sure what I was worried about. This might actually be fun.

Although fun is not exactly the word that runs through my mind four hours later, when I'm covered in sweat and my feet are raw. And this is just the beginning.

We've got to work on the ensemble piece of the dance now.

Kori consults her schedule. "Let's break for lunch. Make sure to eat and hydrate, and we'll meet back here at two."

I flex and extend my toes, trying to get some feeling back in them, but knowing the moment it returns, it'll be sharp, stinging pain. While the dancing and the aerial work has kept me fit, my feet have had a break for the summer. And they're going to make me pay for it now.

"I think I'm going to dance this afternoon in my soft shoes," I tell Melinda. Her feet, gnarled and calloused, have been spared open wounds. "I haven't been on pointe in a few weeks, and my feet got soft." Most people assume that ballet dancers, who look so beautiful while dancing, have beautiful feet as well. It's quite the opposite. That beauty exacts a toll on us.

She nods, knowing what I'm going through. She reaches into her bag and hands me a roll-on tube of Tiger Balm which I use on my arches. "Thanks. Mine's up in my room." I didn't have time to grab it this morning after waking up so late with Josh.

Josh.

The mere thought of last night makes a small smile dance across my lips. I hope he's at lunch. Suddenly, I've got a little more energy to pull myself together to get up to the dorms.

But on the way up the hill, I start to think. If there was an award for overthinking, surely, I would win that one. Things were good, up until I had that small freak out about people possibly finding out about us. I could probably also win an award for messing things up.

I'll just tell Josh that I'm still working things out in my head, and the pressure of everyone else having expectations for us is too much to deal with. Surely he'll be okay with the fact that I need a little distance, at least in public, for right now.

As soon as I enter the dining room, I feel his eyes trained on me. I give him a quick glance with a hint of a smile, before turning to Melinda to show her where things are located. "Who's that cutie?" She elbows me. "The guy with the great hair. I saw him earlier and wanted to ask. Well, first off, is he straight?"

I follow her gaze. Of course, she's looking at Josh. I wish I could tell her just how hetero he is. "Josh is our musical director. You'll get to work with him a lot."

"Yumm-o," she says. "I think singing just got bumped up to being my favorite thing." She glances over her shoulder at Max, who's already hitting on unsuspecting chorus girls. "I mean, Max is pretty to look at, but he doesn't bring a whole lot more than that to the table. Know what I mean?"

Unfortunately, I do. She looks back to Josh and smiles at him.

Jealousy roils through me. As if it's not enough that she has my part—the part I was literally *born* to play— now she wants my man? Hell to the no.

I mean, she doesn't know he's my man. And I can't let her know that either.

Oh shit. This is all sorts of confusing in my brain. Like trigonometry or trying to figure out the plot to *Lost*. I look at my still empty plate and am tempted to walk away.

Tempted, but I don't do it.

Not eating will not change my job status at The Edison. It will not change Max from being the conceited prick that he is. It will not make my relationship with Josh easier.

Food has nothing to do with any of it.

And I can't really control any of those things either.

All I can do is take a deep breath and try to put one foot in front of the other. I put a scoop of tuna salad on a bed of lettuce and tomatoes. I add a slice of bread. Looking down at my full plate, I smile. I may actually figure this out. Putting lunch on a dish may not seem like a big feat, but for me, I feel like I climbed Mount Everest.

Now if I could just figure out how to process my feelings about Josh. It would be easy to say I'm in love with him, but I'm not sure that's possible. I'm not sure I'm ready for that yet. I want to be. I wish I was. Yet somehow I know I've got a lot of heavy lifting left to do before I can be the person he needs me to be.

I've betrayed his trust by deserting him once before. A wave of guilt crashes over me when I think about the devastating loss he suffered. And I let him go through it on his own. I can't do that to him again. So no matter what, I have to be upfront and honest with him about where I am in our relationship. About where I am in my relationship with myself. I glance up to see Josh's gaze trained on me. I look away. I have to tell him before I hurt him again.

I'll talk to him as soon as lunch is done. I hurry to scarf down my food and then run to brush my teeth before the afternoon. The tuna was delicious, but no one wants to be smelling it as our faces are close together, dancing in partner.

Coming down out of my room, I'm not surprised to see Josh waiting for me. Good. "I know we have to get back to rehearsal." I pull out my phone to see that it's almost two. I wish the hours of dancing and staging could fly by as quickly as the breaks do. "But can I say something?"

Josh nods, taking my hands in his. "Anything." He looks so hopeful.

"Josh, last night was great. It really was. And I've been thinking about it for ten years, so it says a lot that it lived up to the hype." I pause, thinking about it. "Actually, it exceeded it."

He smiles and leans in, giving me a slow, sensuous kiss that promises a lot more surpassed expectations. "I'm glad to hear it."

"But I think our timing is still sucky. I mean, I'm just starting to have breakthroughs with Malachi, and then there's this." I wave my hand around to indicate our surroundings. "I want to be with you. I care for you so much; more than you'll ever know, but I'm not sure I can also handle the weight of everyone's expectations and judgments. And I know they shouldn't matter, but it's something I'm still dealing with."

Josh's hands drop. "So tell me what you want. What you need."

I don't know the answers. "I need to figure me out a little more before we go public. That's it. I need time."

"So we're back to sneaking around like we did when we were teenagers?"

I run my finger up his arm. "It could be fun." He stiffens. I let my hand fall away. Maybe he thinks last night was a mistake. Was it a mistake? Does he wish we weren't involved again? Is he still mad at me? I'd be mad at me if I were him. Hell, I've spent my whole life sort of hating myself. It's like my default setting. Why wouldn't it be his too?

I need to give him an out. I know what pressure is like, and I'm not going to do that to him. "Or we could just cool it for a few weeks until there's less going on, ya know? More time. It's not like we're leaving camp and will never see each other. We both live in the city. Hell, I think we both live in Brooklyn even. Surely, we can figure something out then. Later. In the fall." I shrug, trying to be casual. "Or whenever. Or not."

"So you're saying ..." His voice is cold.

I continue rambling. "I'm not sure if I can do this right now. Be there for you, like you need me to be. I can barely be there for me."

What's he thinking?

His face becomes hard and distant. Regret. That's what's written all over his face. He wishes last night didn't happen. My stomach drops, and that tuna threatens a massive U-turn.

"It's no big deal. We don't have to be anything."

I guess that's that.

Chapter 28: Josh

Very rarely in my life have I regretted sleeping with someone. In fact, it's only happened twice. Unfortunately, it's been with the same person each time.

I should have known Leslie wasn't ready. That she still can't be there for me when I need her. That it's still on her timeline.

And maybe she'll never be there for me.

She wants to either hide or cool it until the end of the season. "Yeah, sure. Fine. Whatever you want. I, uh, better get back to rehearsal. See you there."

I turn to walk away.

I haven't even told her about *Honor Code* yet. It's the biggest thing in my life, but I've been reluctant to share the news with her. To trust her with it. Which means she doesn't know that I'm not returning to the city in September after the season ends. I might head down for gigs and the like, crashing with D'von when I need to, but otherwise, I'm making my home base up here in Hicklam.

It only makes sense, since it looks as if Tabitha is relocating here permanently. And she wants to be very hands-on with this production. Who am I to say no to that?

I'm literally on the cusp of my dreams, and to channel my inner Elphaba, no one's gonna bring me down.

Let's face it, it's probably not the right time for me to take on a relationship either. I still need to put together two numbers for Tabitha to see. I was going to ask Leslie to help choreograph them, but now I don't know that she wants to be around me that much. And if I can't touch her, look at her, *love her*, I might as well stay away.

Looks like I'll ask Kori to choreograph for me instead.

As the week drags on, I can't decide if it's worse to be completely ghosted, where they seem to vanish off the face of the earth, or to have to see that other person every single day. Laughing. Talking. Touching.

The touching is driving me crazy. It's the theater world. I get it. They live by a different set of rules than the rest of the world. They are bonded by acting, and that familiarity has to be forged quickly. A lot of that is done through touch. And as I see the ballet dancing come together, there's a large, rational part of me that understands the need for the contact.

Yet there's a small, quite irrational, quite loud part of my brain that is screaming every time Max's hands are on Leslie's arm. Or her back. Or her inner thighs.

Especially her inner thighs.

His arrogance is staggering, even for this environment. Every time he walks into the room, I want to roll my eyes. I'm starting to feel like Henderson. Basically, I don't like him, and though I've never been the violent sort, the way he's always touching Leslie makes me want to deck the prick.

It bothers me with Braedyn too, but not as much. Leslie's not his type. As in, she's female. But still, he gets to hold her, be close to her, and feel her in all the ways I can't right now.

Maybe, I tell myself, *I don't really feel this deeply about her.* Maybe it's because she's the forbidden fruit that she seems so appealing. Maybe I'm not going to get my heart broken by this woman for the second time.

I'm a dreamer, but even I'm not that foolish.

Because every night, I wait for her to slip into my room. To slip into my bed. To give me something besides the small smile she gives everyone. Yet there's nothing from her.

So every night, as my door is left unlocked just in case, I do the only thing I can to keep my mind occupied. I work on my show. Tweaking lyrics, layering orchestrations, rewriting scenes. I'm not sleeping, and eating has become perfunctory. I need to keep moving. Keep busy.

Anything to keep from thinking about her. But that's easier said than done when I spend most of the day in her proximity. I'm so glad this show isn't music-heavy. She's got to learn the ensemble bits of course, but Lise only has a few songs to sing.

And when I return to my room, the book for my show has taken on a life of its own. A story of betrayal. Because of not being honest with herself about who she really is, Dawn ends up betraying Oliver, the man in love with her. The man she claims to love.

Art imitating life much?

Although it's not like we're at the love stage, because how could we be? I don't even know her. Hell, *she* doesn't know herself. Not yet.

Even if she doesn't see herself clearly, I see her. I see that small spark of light, growing brighter every day as she lets go of the weight of the expectations that have defined her whole life. And the last thing she needs is me, pressing down upon her, pinning her to the ground when she's just figuring out how to fly.

I can let her be. It's not like I have a choice—I'm not one of those dicks who would keep hounding her after she said she wasn't ready. I only wish she'd thought about this before we slept together again. It took me years to get over her before. Now I have new memories, new sensations burning into my brain. I need to let her go.

I get up and lock my door.

Chapter 29: Leslie

I can't believe my life right now. Who would've thought that letting go of my dream and my expectations to be the best would have resulted in actual happiness?

With Malachi's help, I've realized that the philosophy of "whatever it takes" costs a lot more than it's worth. So what if I'm not a principal ballerina? I'm still performing. I'm doing what I love and hearing that applause at the end of the show.

I came into this thinking I'd lost. Yet with The Edison, I've found so much more. There's a level of acceptance here that I've never felt, not even in New York City. Levi was right—we are all the misfit toys, but together, we make the most awesome set. I'm learning and growing, and I don't feel like I'm pounding on that same brick wall until my knuckles are bloody and it still won't let me pass. No, now that I've begun to accept myself, doors are starting to open.

And then there's Josh.

I'm sure it's my imagination that things are a little strained since we slept together. The timing on it was just the worst possible. I'm so exhausted, physically and mentally, from the rehearsals that once I get to my room, I've got nothing left for him. I get out of the shower, and most nights fall asleep still in my robe, not possessing the energy to even get dressed, let alone walk down the hall to hang out with him.

As soon as this show is done, we'll have plenty of time. Forever, maybe even. I can imagine telling people at The Edison how we met when we were sixteen. Fast friends and first loves, reunited back in the theater.

If you'd asked me six months ago, I would never have been able to predict this happy ending for myself.

However, there's one thing left I need to do before I can really start moving on. I dread this, which is why I've put it off so long. I take my lunch break and decide that this is the day to do it. I walk to one of the garden benches for some privacy and take out my phone.

Time to call my sister.

"Hey, Mer, how's things?"

"Busy." I should be used to my sister's clipped tone. We're not close. We haven't ever really been. We were always too different.

"Yeah, here too. I don't know if Mom or Dad told you, but I'm working with a musical theater now. It's north of the city in this quaint little town called Hicklam. I sort of love it." It's true.

"That's nice. So are you done with ballet?"

"I guess. Although I'm in *An American in Paris*, so that's all ballet. But in terms of a company, yes. That chapter's closed." I run my fingers over the wrought-iron scrollwork on the end of the bench. I never thought I'd be able to say that without it hurting, but it doesn't.

"I never thought I'd see the day. Ballet was all you cared about." Her tone carries years of hurt.

"It's not all I cared about." I'm lying. I would have sold everything I had for a chance to succeed. You could say I did sell my self-worth for a chance. I realize how disordered that way of thinking was. "I care about you."

With the background noise, it's hard to tell, but I'm pretty sure she "hmphs" at me.

"What are you doing?" I ask. "It sounds like you're in a wind tunnel."

"I am. I'm in Chicago for a conference, and I had to step out to take your call. You never call, so I figured something bad had happened."

As much as I hate to admit it, she has a point. "No, I'm just … re-prioritizing things. I wanted to check in with you just because."

"Well, that's great that you finally think you have time for me. Turns out, I'm busy. I'll talk to you later."

She's about to hang up; I can tell. I haven't made much progress with making amends and repairing this relationship. "Meri, wait! I hoped we could catch up."

"I'm busy. You have your life, I have mine." After a quick goodbye, she disconnects.

Well, that was terrible. Why can't we be like Josh and his sister? What's Malachi going to have to say about this? Is he going to make me call her again? We don't have a very sisterly relationship. We never have. Not since she dropped out of ballet class when I was six and she was eight. After that, our lives moved down two totally different paths.

And she hated—*hates*—me because I picked ballet. Because I excelled at it. I think she wanted to do it too, but she had two left feet. I wasn't the only one who heard the teacher ask how it was possible that we were even related. Ballet is the only thing I've ever been better at than her. Not grades, not friends, not boys, not life.

There's no way she can be holding that against me. Not after all these years.

I redial my sister. "Is this because of what Miss Kristi said all those years ago in ballet class? Is that why you hate me?"

"No. And I told you, I'm at a conference."

Oh shit. I forgot. I drop my voice to a whisper, like that really matters. She's on her cell phone. Unless she's got me on speaker, my volume isn't the problem.

"Please, Meri, I just want an answer."

"Of course you do. Because it's always all about you. Like your ballet class and your shoes and your costumes and your lessons. And let's not forget your eating disorder. Your anorexia needs its own place at our dinner table. I mean, not really, because we all know neither of you eat. My entire life was about what worked for *you*. What *Leslie* needed. It was never about me."

Her words sting. Mostly because they're probably true.

I go on the defensive. "It's not like I decided it would be cool to hate myself so much that I thought that would be the best thing. You know, to try to deprive myself of fuel and nutrients, just so I could *maybe* look the way they wanted me to look, even though that was never gonna happen. I was always going to be short and muscular. I was always gonna have boobs and the badonkadonk in the back. I was always going to be the wrong color." I was always gonna hate myself. "Ballet, the thing I loved more than anything, made me hate the person I was. I think it took as much from me as it gave me. And I'm not sure that sacrifice was worth it."

There's silence on the line.

Just like I can't make myself be better than my best, I can't make Meri accept my apology. I can't make her accept me. "I won't keep you from your conference and your life. I just wanted to see if I could have a sister one of these days."

I disconnect.

Somehow, I don't feel any better. Aren't I supposed to feel better? But what I said was true. All those things I sacrificed were for something that made me hate who I was. For as much as ballet gave me, it exacted a high toll. The desire to be the best ... whatever it takes ... was too high a price to pay.

Some things aren't worth it.

But some things are. Like Josh.

And then I realize I'm doing it again. I'm pouring everything I have into this production without leaving anything for me. For those I ... love. And I do love him. I love his smile and how he conducts music with his eyebrows. I love his delicate touch and his sensitive perception. I love how he smells when my head is buried in his chest. I love that he cares about the people around him. I love watching his fingers glide over the piano keys, creating the most beautiful music. I love how his mouth feels on mine. But mostly, I love that he understands me and doesn't judge me.

I stand up, shocked by this revelation. As an adult, I've never been in love. I wasn't capable of it. I had to start loving who I was before I could love another.

Almost as shocking as the revelation about my feelings for Josh are my feelings for myself. I don't think I'm all the way cured or healed or whole or whatever, but in this moment, I *accept*.

I accept me and all the things that come with it, good and bad. I accept that my best wasn't *the* best, and that it's okay.

I head toward the music room, where I'm sure to find him. I need to tell Josh. I need to take the time and the energy and the mental space to give him what he needs.

That thought halts me in my tracks. I don't know what he wants. Or needs. Everything's been ... about me.

My sister is right. I'm selfish. I can't even see how my actions hurt because I take and I take and I take. I'm not doing it to be mean or petty. It's just that my well of need was bottomless, so I relied on others to fill it up. All because I wasn't strong enough to fill it myself.

Fill your own well.

Now *that* would make a good T-shirt.

Maybe instead of rushing in there to tell Josh I'm ready, I should approach it differently. Maybe I should see what *he* needs. Be his partner. His equal.

Quietly, I approach the music room. I slow down when I hear his voice. "I've been up every night this week working on it. It's done. At least the first version."

"What numbers are you going to show Tabitha?" Henderson's accent is unmistakable. I pause, trying to figure out what they're talking about.

"Definitely 'Purple Dawn' and probably 'Look at Me.' What do you think about those?" There's a ruffling sound that's obviously paper.

"I agree on the ballad, and 'Look at Me' seems fun. What are you going to do about choreo and the like?"

"I was going to ask Leslie, but I don't know that she's up for it. I talked to Kori this morning."

His words are like a punch to my gut.

"Right. You need to bring your A-game. This'll be Tabitha's last chance to decide how much she's going to fund, so you have to show her what you can do. It's got to be your best."

"That's what I'm hoping for, the best. Kori and I'll knock it out of the park."

I sink to the floor, grief and pain washing over me in waves. He doesn't want me because I'm not the best. It's my biggest fear realized. Once again, no matter how hard I work, it's not enough.

I sit there, knees to my chest, and will the tears to stay away. I listen to the beautiful music Josh is playing. It's nothing I've ever heard before.

And then everything makes sense. *His show*.

Tabitha Stetson is funding his show. It's going to happen. He's auditioning numbers for her. These songs he's written that Kori will choreograph. They'll be performed and will either make or break his career.

And I'm not good enough to do that for him.

The old Leslie would storm in, demanding to know how she could do better. The old Leslie would insist on another chance. The old Leslie would berate and beat herself up with a series of "if onlys."

Okay, there might be a tiny bit of internal self-flagellation going on. There's a reason why they say that old habits die hard. But I'm trying to learn. I owe it to myself to grow and be better.

To be the best Leslie I can be.

And the best Leslie has to find a way to make it up to Josh.

Chapter 30: Josh

It's Leslie's night to play Lise.

I get to stare at her for three hours and no one will think anything of it. This past week, with my resolve to move on, I've tried not to look. Not to think. Not to feel.

It's made me miserable.

Even as I'm working with Kori and Braedyn and Marcelina to bring my view of *Honor Code* to life, I can't stop thinking about her. Wishing it were her in this room, dancing to my music.

Tonight's her night to take center stage.

I've been milling about for fifteen minutes now, trying to resist the urge to visit her backstage before the show. To wish her luck, obviously, and nothing more.

Because she has no room to give me anything more. I can't ask because she can't give. Once again, our timing is terrible. Maybe someday it will work out.

Or maybe it'll be the third strike.

I'm not much into baseball, but even I know enough not to swing at an outside pitch. And that's what staying involved with her would be. Swinging haphazardly with no hope of a home run.

Okay, I'm out of sports metaphors. I am a musician after all.

"Chookas," I hear Henderson saying as he leaves Leslie's dressing room. "Howdy, mate," he says to me, passing in the hall. I nod and rush to her door, tapping lightly before I lose my courage.

I've been trying to formulate what to say to her for a week now. Trying to tell her that she broke my heart—again—but I was trying to be adult enough to understand why. Trying to tell her that she's not ready for a relationship, and it was foolish to think we should try again. Trying to tell her that my dreams are finally becoming a reality, and maybe someday she can wish me well, as I'm about to wish her.

Instead, I say, "What's chookas?"

Leslie turns, almost unrecognizable in a black, bobbed wig. "Oh, Josh. I didn't expect you."

"What's chookas?" I repeat, apparently unable to form any other words.

"It's Australian for good luck in the ballet theater. Most of the time, we just say merde, but you know, it's Henderson, so ..." She looks at me, painted red lips plump.

I run my hands through my hair and then shove them deep in my pockets. "Well, break a leg. That's all I came to say too." I turn to leave.

"Josh?" Her voice is faint, almost a whisper.

I give her a tight smile, my back teeth grinding together. I want nothing more than to sweep her into my arms and ruin that lipstick. Instead, I clench my molars harder, balling my hands into tight fists. "I've got to go warm up. You'll do great out there."

I walk away. That could've gone better. I take my place in the pit. I long for the days when I not only had to play and conduct and direct, but mix sound as well, because I'd be able to pull on my headphones and cancel out the world around me.

I really do need to focus. Gershwin's music is timeless and classic—and well known. The audience knows what they're hearing, even if they don't know it coming in. We have to be on the mark. I've been distracted—to say the least—this week. I have to hope my musicians don't let me down.

But the moment Jen starts wailing on her alto sax during the overture— the immediately recognizable melody of this show—I know we've got this. I make a mental note to make sure I've got a sax solo somewhere for Jen to play in my show.

And then Leslie steps out on stage, and I almost forget what I'm doing. Even though with the wig and makeup she's barely recognizable, the moment she starts dancing, I *know* her. How she moves. Her soul. Everything in my body yearns for her.

Watching her, I feel a heavy tug in my chest. As proud as I am of her, I know this won't make her happy. It's not what she wanted. She settled by coming here in the first place, and even now is playing second fiddle. She's truly great at this, but is she the best?

What is the best? Is it something unattainable like a quest in some Greek myth? Will she spend the rest of her life like Sisyphus, pushing the rock up the mountain only to have it roll back down again? There's not room for two of us there, rolling that rock, unless you're willing to get flattened by the boulder time and time again.

And then it happens. Leslie looks out at me and smiles. Sure, her character is smiling, but this one's for me. I can't help myself. I smile back and give her a little eyebrow lift, trying to tell her I'm proud of her.

Even if she broke my heart, she's still killing it up there. I see that drive. That determination. All that hard work. She is destined to be the best, and I won't stand in her way.

Maybe someday we can go back to being friends. As if I wasn't in love with her from the moment I saw her. Friends—distant friends—it will have to be.

Act One ends with the upbeat "Second Rhapsody" and "Cuban Overture." It's almost eight minutes of music and dancing without dialogue. I'm sweating, but love the piano I get to play, showcasing my talent. I wonder if dancing makes Leslie feel how playing makes me feel.

No wonder she never wants to stop.

At intermission, I lie down on the floor in the music room, stretching my back, shoulders, and arms out, knowing what the second act will bring. The rest of the band is in the large rehearsal space, getting drinks and relaxing for these few minutes. I don't hear Tabitha come in.

"Okay, so I gotta know, what's the deal with you and Leslie?" She sits down on the floor cross-legged next to me.

I lift my head up off the floor. "I don't know what you mean."

She waves a hand at me. "Josh, don't kid a kidder. I see those looks between the two of you. Those *meaningful glances*. I also see that you're trying not to look at her and have avoided her the past week or so. What's that all about?"

I rest my head back down and close my eyes. "It's nothing. We're friends."

Lie.

"Friends. Right. Like Henderson and I are friends?"

I open one eye. "I don't know what goes on behind closed doors. Maybe you're playing Uno."

"What's going on, as you very well know, is much more of a duo thing. But I see you. I saw you at the cabaret, watching her. And I saw that smile she gave you, and how you returned it. You both might as well have hearts coming out of your eyes."

I roll to my side, propping up on my elbow, resting my head on my hand. "What can I say? Our timing is terrible. Once again."

This has her sitting up straight. "Once again?"

Shit.

"I guess I let that cat out of the bag." I can't help but make a cat joke. Tabitha does all the time. "Leslie and I went to drama camp together when we were sixteen. It was ..." I don't know how to describe it. Those eight weeks were such a bright point before the darkness and devastation that followed. "Poor timing," I offer lamely.

"And you still love each other!" Tabitha clasps her hands to her chest. "Oh, that's so wonderful. You should write a show about the two of you."

In a way, I already have.

I shake my head. "No, it's still not the right time. She's going through a lot. Like years of stuff that she's just beginning to sort through. And until she's through it, I can't be with her. I'm only going to get hurt again while she's figuring herself out."

Tabitha stands up, shaking her head. I move to a sitting position. "You know, Josh, with how you went balls to the wall trying to sell your show, I didn't have you pegged for a coward. If you wait for the perfect time, it'll never come. And if you think you can love without the risk of getting hurt, then you'll never know what love actually is."

Chapter 31: Leslie

Here it is, the ballet scene. A fourteen-minute dance segment that has me—my character, that is—dreaming that her dance partner is really the artist she's in love with.

I wonder if Josh can dance?

But instead, I start dancing with Braedyn, who's quickly replaced by Max. I'm on stage and dancing for almost twelve of the fourteen minutes, including two costume changes. I start to panic that I'm not going to pull it off. The saxophones begin to wail the melody and I want to freeze.

However, once Max pulls me into his arms for the first time, I'm assured I'll be fine. Whether I want to admit it or not, Max and I move well together. He's very talented. Maybe not in the bedroom so much, but certainly as a dancer, actor, and singer. He really is a triple threat.

His arms are sturdy during the lifts and holds, making me feel light as a feather. His large hands span my ribcage as if I'm a waif. In that instant, I feel beautiful. In reality, it's another story.

Both of us are sweating like stuffed pigs and trying not to let the exertion show on our faces. I can't even think about the choreography; it flows right through me. If I have to stop and think about it, I'll lose where I am. Instead, I rely on muscle memory and the power of the music to tell my body what to do. Max pulls me into an embrace—a kiss—and I know I'm in the home stretch.

If only Max were Josh. Involuntarily, my eyes dart toward the pit. He's not even watching me.

Do your best. Be your best. My brain chants this over and over. This is a subtle, yet different, narrative than I've told myself my whole life. Replacing the word "the" with "your" has been a game-changer.

And I know I'm up here, doing my best.

The only thing that could make this night better would be to celebrate with Josh.

As the show draws to its conclusion, I'm clad in the iconic yellow dress, and Max and I walk, arms around each other, as if we're heading into the Paris painted on the backdrop. The curtain falls.

I did it.

I starred in *An American in Paris*. As we take our bows, it's all I can do not to cry. It doesn't matter that this is a small theater. It doesn't matter that I'm not backed by a famous ballet company.

I still did it.

And with friends who care about me. Family too. I spy my parents in the audience, on their feet and clapping wildly. I bow, a slight curtsy, before taking

Max's hand and bowing again. We lift our arms and drop them toward the pit so that everyone can applaud the band.

The music is another star of this show, and Josh deserves every single clap that's coming his way. He's so talented. He's going to make it, I just know it.

I spy Tabitha in the wings. Josh really is going to make it, with Tabitha's backing. Not that he's told me. Pain pangs my heart, penetrating this moment. Josh is on his feet, looking toward the audience. Away from me. Like I don't exist.

I close my eyes for the briefest of seconds, before opening them and waving one last time at the audience. Max is holding my hand and we back up as the curtain falls. In a moment of rare sincerity, Max squeezes my hand and pulls me into an embrace.

"You were great." If I didn't know better, I'd say there was a hint of surprise in his voice. As if, despite all the rehearsals, he didn't know that I'd actually be able to do it.

"Thanks." I should tell him he was great too, but I don't need to feed his ego at all. He already knows it. I break the embrace and head to the backstage area. I need to find my parents.

My face hurts from smiling, thanking each of the cast and crew who stop me to offer their congratulations and praise. Gloria appears, pulling me into a hug. This is big. She doesn't come to many shows, so I know she was there for me.

"Girl, you killed it up there. Magical. Absolutely magical. Henderson should be shot for not casting you directly."

I shrug, not sure how to respond to it. "I'm trying to let it go and work on the philosophy that things happen for a reason." To give up the desire to control things that I can't. And not to take it out on myself.

"Yeah, well, don't make any plans to go anywhere anytime soon. We're not going to let you go."

I wish Josh felt the same way. I see him down the hall, relaxed and laughing with some members of the band. He's relaxed without me. He doesn't need me.

Maybe he doesn't even want me.

But then his gaze drifts up and meets mine, and I feel it deep in my gut. The want, the need, the *connection* is there. His hazel eyes are full of ... pain.

Pain that I've caused. I'm not even sure what I did, but I know I'm responsible. Suddenly my high is dampened. How can I enjoy this moment knowing that I've hurt someone I care so much about?

Someone that I love.

Suddenly, none of this matters. The applause, the accolades, the dance. None of it matters if I'm hurting Josh. If I can't make him happy, then it's not worth it.

I need to tell him this. I start down the hall, but there are people in my way. I feel like a salmon trying to swim upstream. For every person I get through, there's someone else standing there. At one point in my life, this was all I ever wanted.

To know that I was the best.

Now it seems so trivial. So frivolous.

"Thank you," I offer, smiling. "Thank you," I say to the next person. Where's Josh? How many more people before I get to him? But then I'm at the end of the hall, and he's gone.

I missed him.

I keep searching, heading back toward the stage. To the pit. Out to the audience.

"Leslie!" I turn. The voice calling my name is not Josh's, but my mom's. In my haste to find him, I'd forgotten they were here.

My dad pulls me into a tight hug. "Great job, honey."

Now it's my mom's turn to hug me. "You were the best!"

I cringe slightly at her words. She doesn't mean harm; she just doesn't know the pressure, the weight they carry. "I worked very hard."

I'm not going to use the "b" word.

Mom nods. "It shows. Maybe next year, you'll get cast as the lead. If you just put in a little more—"

"You must be Mr. and Mrs. Moose. Nice to meet you. I'm Josh deChambeau, the musical director here." Josh sweeps in, offering a hearty handshake to both my dad and my mom. "Leslie's been a huge asset to The Edison this year. I'm not sure that we would have made it without her fantastic performance earlier this season in *The Greatest Showman*." He looks at me and offers a tight smile. "She was a sight to behold."

I smile gratefully at Josh. "Remember that summer I went to STP? Josh was there. He was my only friend there."

"Leslie was always too focused on ballet to have a lot of friends," my mom offers, excusing my behavior.

I'm about to jump in and defend myself when Josh says curtly, "Yes, I'm aware how much being the best means to Leslie. And what she's willing to sacrifice along the way."

His words sting, and instantly I blink back the tears filling my eyes.

"Now if you'll excuse me, I have to go."

He doesn't even make up some lame excuse—he simply can't wait to get away from me. He's still mad. Or mad again. He has every right to be. I pulled him close, only to push him away so I could focus on what's *important* to me. In other words, not him.

He must feel that everything in my life is more important to me than he is.

Yet even as mad at me as he is, he still steps in to defend me. He's shown me over and over how I should treat him—how I should make him a priority—but I've been too stupid and self-absorbed to see it. Josh is just as committed to The Edison as anyone else here, not to mention his own actual show. But he still had time for me, if I had taken him up on it.

He knows how to balance. He knows how to prioritize. He knows what's important. For the first time in my life, I could walk away from all of this. Ballet no longer has a stranglehold on me, like a gaslighting partner. I'd never dance again if Josh would forgive me.

He's more important.

I'm more important. Me as a whole person. The best person I can be.

So now it's time to win Josh back, whatever it takes.

Chapter 32: Josh

It's not right. The song. This damned, infernal song. The power ballad, the turning point. And it's not right.

"No, no, NO! Stop. You all need to stop. It's terrible." Kori looks at me. Jasmine looks at me. Marcelina looks at me.

I look back.

I've got nothing.

All I know is it's not working.

We've got approximately two hours to finish the choreography for this song before we have to run through *Paris*. It's already Wednesday, and I'm running out of time. The Edison's season officially ends on Sunday, at which time the cast and crew will leave.

I've got to show these two numbers to Tabitha prior to that. With two shows on Saturday, that pretty much leaves Friday for the informal workshop.

"Okay, let's take five," Kori finally calls.

"We don't have time to take five," I practically growl.

"Josh, baby, you take five, or you're gonna find yourself doing all the singing and dancing because we're going to leave your perfectionist ass to do this on your own." Kori walks out of the room. I get glares from Jasmine and Marcelina that back up that sentiment.

Okay, so maybe I'm being a little harsh. And a huge dick. I sort of have to be. If Tabitha doesn't like it, then the last five—ten—years of my life have been wasted. If she does like it, well, then my career is finally starting. I sit at the piano, staring at the music. Do I make that note higher? Add a harmony line?

No, that's not it.

Despair crashes down on me like a wave at high tide. A fitting analogy, since I feel like I'm drowning. I haven't felt this way since my parents died. So lost, grasping for something to pull me back in. I yank out my phone to call Kim—my lifeline—but get her voicemail.

I stand up from the piano bench and pace around the room to see if it helps. It doesn't. If I were a more aggressive type, I'd smash something. If I were more of a dance type, I'd pour my frustration into explosive dance moves, surely worthy of the most epic dance fight scene.

I can't do that either, so I lie down on the floor and try to meditate. I try to empty my brain so that some kind of inspiration can float in and magically give me the answers to this mess.

I've never been very good at meditating. I feel the hard floor under my back. I hear the voices out in the hall, including Jasmine swearing a blue streak in Spanish. I don't actually speak Spanish, but even I know those words and who they're directed at.

My head is pounding. Maybe my brain's about to explode and I won't have to worry about this. Maybe they'll even produce my show, shades of Jonathan Larson's *Rent*, and I'll posthumously be a critical success. It actually seems like a good option at this moment.

The pounding and throbbing continue until I realize it's not in my head, but outside of it. The drums. The beat. I stand up, following the rhythm. I know what it is before I even open the door.

Leslie's in the middle of the room, dancing to the Polynesian—Fijian—music. Gloria's perched on a stool, watching intently. This time, Leslie's hair is slicked back into a low ponytail with a thick braid trailing down. No chance of it springing free like the last time. While her hair may be restrained, her dancing is not.

It's free and joyful and full of pride. She's beaming, radiant. Or maybe that's the sheen of perspiration. As I look at her, everything snaps into place. What I need. What I need to do. Before she can see me and stop, as she does whenever I enter the room these days, I close the door and hurry back to the large dance studio.

I don't have much time, but I've got to rewrite this whole number. I scribble furiously, afraid the inspiration—the vision—will fade off like the morning fog. Kori returns to the room, leaning over my shoulder. I'm not sure how she can decipher the chicken scratch, but she stands for a long moment, trying to process.

Finally, she says, "You keep working. I'll start to map it out in my head, but get me what you can as soon as you can. I think I see where you're heading."

I look at her, my eyes taking a moment to focus on her face rather than the sheet music and the notes that still appear to be dancing in my vision. "Can you see it?"

Kori nods. "I think I know right where you're going with it."

"It sort of means a rewrite."

"Not all of it. Just of some of it. And this is going to make it stronger. Deeper."

"It wasn't supposed to be deep. Oscar Wilde wrote his play purposefully to be trivial."

"And Josh deChambeau will improve on that with a musical that not only has impossible-to-forget songs, but is a commentary on social media, society, and being true to yourself."

I swallow. If I can get this to work—*if*—then Kori's right. I could be on the cusp of something truly important. "I hope Tabitha can see it too."

"Even if she can't see it like I can, she trusts you. She knows how talented you are and that you'll deliver. Now get back to work. We've got to rehearse in a little while. We can do this tomorrow. It'll be fine."

I take a deep breath. "From your lips to God's ears," I mutter. I hope Kori's right.

I really need her to be.

Chapter 33: Leslie

I need your help." Kori finds Gloria and me in the small rehearsal space. Instantly, I'm interested. Kori's been working with Josh all day on his big project—the one he still hasn't told me about. Probably because he's not speaking to me other than when absolutely necessary.

"Sure, we're about done in here." I nod toward Gloria. "I was showing her something for next year. We're thinking about doing *Moana*. It'd be awesome if we could have some authentic Polynesian dancing in it."

They're thinking about doing Moana. *Not* we. *I'm not part of a we.*

Gloria smiles. "I'm only proposing *Moana* for the kids' show if Leslie is here to do it."

My knees start to go a little weak, melting at the implication. "You mean you might want me to come back and help next summer?"

Gloria glances at Kori. "I was thinking something a little more. Like you taking over the camp. Or at least partnering with us on it."

I wrinkle my brows. "What do you mean 'partner?' I'm not following."

I'm also surprised when Kori speaks. "I won't be coming back to The Edison next year. My girlfriend wants to move to LA for her career, so I'm going to head to the West coast and see if I can choreo out there."

"What does that have to do with me?"

"My girlfriend and I own a small dance studio in Hicklam. We generally work with The Edison on getting kids to join the camp. Sometimes we host events, like master classes, during the year to keep the ties to The Edison strong. Today's novices are tomorrow's cast."

I'm blown away. I realize what this means not only to Kori but to Gloria and The Edison. It's huge.

"With Mol and me moving to Cali, we're going to need someone to run the dance studio. Maybe teach some ballet classes."

I clasp my hands to my chest and begin jumping up and down, squealing in an octave I didn't know I could reach. I should remain polished and put together, but this is the biggest thing that's ever happened to me.

I'm more excited about this than I was when I got temporarily promoted at FBBC. Mostly because I know they want *me* for *me*. I'm not a substitute. I'm not a last resort.

"You could even buy us out," Kori adds.

That makes me laugh. "I don't have that kind of money."

"Maybe eventually you could buy us out ... but for now, run the studio. You'd draw a salary and everything. And then you're here," she waves her hand, showing off like Vanna White, "to work with and for The Edison."

I really have lost all ability to form words. Despite my reprieve this summer, my parents have been hinting that I should return to Ohio. And without a concrete plan, I was running out of excuses—and ways to finance—staying in New York.

After all, I couldn't really tell them I wanted to keep my room in Brooklyn on the off chance that Josh forgives me for being so crappy and wants to be with me again. If I'm here in Hicklam, I'll get to be near Josh for at least half of the year.

But teaching?

Those who can, do. Those who can't, teach.

I shake my head, trying to get rid of that internal voice that is so used to telling me I'm not good enough and not right. I've had tons of dance teachers over the years. Some great, some not so much. I focus on those who've made a lasting impression—a positive one, that is—on my life. Miss Margie. Miss Charlene. Miss Gwen. Miss Jillian. I could be that for some little girl—or boy. I could be that encouraging presence, teaching dance while imparting the gift of which I've only recently attained possession.

Self-love.

And now that I can finally love myself, I know I'm ready to love someone else.

"Okay, I'm in," I say.

Kori smiles. Gloria tilts her head slightly. "For what part?"

"Yes. All of it. Whatever you've got for me, I'm game to try. I might not be the best, but I'll give it my best."

Gloria's smile is easy and wide. She pulls me into a hug. "This is gonna be great. I'm finally gonna have someone to hang out with besides Grayson or his mom."

"Don't forget Henderson. He's a ball of fun," Kori says dryly.

"He's not, but Tabitha Stetson is. As soon as details on Josh's show are hammered out, the three of us are hanging out." Gloria nods at me.

"She did promise me a spa day for my badassery during *Showman*," I remember. "Maybe the three of us need to schedule one."

"Now I feel bad that you're leaving me out." Kori pretends to pout.

Gloria waves her off. "You're leaving us for Hollywood. Just remember where you got your start when you're working with Kenny Ortega on the next season of *Julie and the Phantoms*."

"Okay, but before I can go do that, and please God, let Kenny hire me, I've got to get this done for Josh. That's why I came in here. I mean, I needed to talk to you about the studio too, but we're on a time crunch with the Josh thing."

The Josh thing. My stomach does a small flip. I nod, not trusting myself not to blurt out something stupid. Kori pulls out some folded papers that look like they've got hieroglyphics all over them.

"Josh is on the verge of something big here, and this number is the crux of it all. He wants to take the drumbeat of a Polynesian song and layer a piano ballad over it. Of course, he's gonna add in violins and crap like that too, but what he needs is a dancer who can portray both sides. Two different people, all in one. Like a person at war with herself, trying to discover who she really is. I'm a little at a loss on what to do with this. I don't know that style of dance, and I don't have the time to research it."

My mouth goes dry. This is it. This is my chance to make it up to Josh. To prove to him that I'll come through this time and not leave him hanging. "Let me do it! I can choreograph it! I can teach it to whoever you want. I won't let you down."

I won't let Josh down.

Kori smiles. "Who do you want to teach it to? Do you know anyone in the company with both ballet and Polynesian dance experience? Again, we've got like no time."

My heart lifts. He wrote this for me, and I'm going to deliver it to him.

Gloria squeals and claps her hands. "Leslie, she means you."

I turn to look at Gloria because it was pretty clear what Kori meant. "Thanks for that, Captain Obvious." I wink. "Okay, I'm in, but one thing. Josh kind of hates me right now. Is he gonna get pissed if I turn up in this number?"

"Josh doesn't hate anyone. He doesn't have a mean bone in his body." Kori laughs. "He's like, too nice."

"Well, he hates me." Despite that, he's still nice, trying to shield me from the well-intentioned, yet still harsh, words from my mom. "I sort of broke his heart—and his trust—twice." I wince as I say it, the ugly truth shameful.

"Wait, what?" Kori pulls up a chair and sits down. I swear if she had a tub of popcorn she'd start eating it.

I roll my eyes. "Long story short because we don't have any time to spare. Josh and I were … together when we were sixteen and at summer camp. I ghosted him afterward because I was a mess with ballet and my mindset and an eating disorder and everything. I couldn't handle a relationship. However, his parents died in an accident right at that time, so my ghosting was like a double betrayal. Fast forward ten years and we're here together. He doesn't want to like me, but what made us friends to begin with is still there. One thing led to another …" I shrug. "You know how it is. But I told him I'm still trying to figure my shit out, because it's the truth, and I need time. I didn't necessarily mean I didn't want to be with him, but I just didn't want to be public about it. That adds a layer of stress. Especially because I slept with Max once, and he told everyone in the company and implied that I was using it to get ahead, and I don't want people to think I'm doing that with Josh because I would never do that to Josh …" I'm rambling, speaking about a mile a minute.

Kori holds up her hands, motioning for me to stop. "Wait, you and Max hooked up too?"

I shake my head. "We did, like years ago when we were in Five Boroughs together. It was a one-night, quick—and I mean *quick*—wham, bam, thank you, ma'am. But then the douche told everyone the next day like it was his mission to sleep his way through the company, and now he could cross me off the list. But he also made people think that I was trading sexual favors for a chance at advancement."

Gloria practically growls. "I hate guys like that." I know enough of her history to know she has a reason behind that sentiment.

"Honestly, it doesn't bother me anymore. I've got so many other things that are more worthy of my energy. There will always be Maxes in the world. You know, the people who think they're God's gift—and maybe their talent is—but their ability to be a decent human being, not to mention a decent lay, is sorely lacking." And with that, I dissolve into a fit of giggles. Kori and Gloria soon join me.

Wiping the tears from my eyes, I finish with, "But I've left Josh high and dry twice now, both at pivotal moments in his life. First when his parents died, and now with this show. He still hasn't even told me about it. But even if he doesn't want me back, I want to help him. To show him that he matters to me, and that he's worth it. That I can think about someone other than myself." I nod, punctuating the last statement. "So let's get to work here."

Chapter 34: Josh

This is it, my moment of truth. Kori and I spent all day yesterday hammering out the style and choreography. I think she was probably up all night teaching it to Jasmine and Marcelina. Now the moment is here. It's time to show "Purple Dawn" and "Look at Me" to Tabitha. Henderson's flittering about like a nervous aunt. I don't blame him. Tabitha's relaxed and casual, as she usually is. The two of them are like night and day.

He put it all on the line for me and this show. Well, also for Tabitha and his relationship with her. By presenting this show, Tabitha is stepping into a new role as executive producer and director. And while I know she agreed to produce—and fund—my show sight unseen, I need her to know what she's getting into before I accept a dime.

I won't take advantage of her generosity and impulsiveness with a less-than-worthy project. She didn't have to agree to fund this. Hell, she volunteered to do it. I know that's how she rolls, but I still feel the need to prove myself to her.

The success of *Honor Code* could launch most of our careers. Henderson was willing to raise funding himself if only so Tabitha could have a project to work on. He was willing to give her the direction and focus her life lacked.

As stodgy as Henderson can be, Tabitha's certainly brought out a different side of him. I wish I could say the same of Leslie. Maybe she did bring out a different side of me. One who's more cautious. One who doesn't want to be so liberal with his heart, and easy with his smiles.

Even as I glance at my sheet music, I know that's not true. Those are traits I've inherited from my mother, and ones I'm proud to display. Music is, and has always been, my therapy and my escape, and this is no different. With *Honor Code* finally coming to fruition, it'll be a catharsis for me.

It's probably been a good thing that Leslie was here this summer.

But … she's here. *Here*.

Walking into the studio with Kori and Jasmine.

"Where's Marcelina?" I hiss through gritted teeth. I notice Tabitha looking at me, and I try to smile. I'm sure it looks like something out of a bad school picture.

Kori leans over and whispers, "Don't worry. We've got this."

"But …"

"Do you trust me?" Kori cocks her eyebrow, making the ring in it dance.

I don't trust her.

"But ..." I stammer again.

"But nothing. It's good. We've got you." Kori follows my gaze. "She's got you. Don't worry. Let's just get this going so I can take a nap before the show tonight."

That's right. We've still got a performance of *Paris* tonight. Four more in total. This isn't the only thing on the agenda.

I shake my shoulders and sit up straighter.

The percussion section, along with our violinist, Sun Li, are here to accompany me. They too had burned the midnight oil in rehearsing this piece. Lucky for me, they are all skilled and talented musicians with the ability to pick up music quickly, as well as sight-read.

I look to the middle of the dance floor where Jasmine's ready to start. She begins this number, only to be quickly replaced by the woman she's pretending to be—Leslie.

"So in this show, our main character, Dawn, played by Leslie, has been living a double life. Her alter ego, Honor, is a fun-loving carefree spirit, while Dawn tends to a lot of family responsibilities and expectations. We only know and see Honor through her social media profile. Dawn's best friend, Jo Jo, played by Jasmine here, sometimes assumes the Honor persona. But at this point in the story, Dawn is realizing that Honor is much more of who she is at heart, and that it's time to claim that for herself. But she's got to get Jo Jo to stop playing that role first. She does it by telling her true feelings to her best friend. And that's where we are heading into this song, 'Purple Dawn.' Enjoy."

I turn back to the musicians and count them in, the rhythmic beating of Kameron's hands on the leather of the drum filling the studio. Don adds the rain stick and Jasmine begins dancing. Then I start in with the piano and Sun Li on the violin. Leslie walks in slowly, gracefully. With the art her ballet training instilled, she floats across the stage, her words soulful and full of realization. Jasmine keeps in time to the beat of the drums while Leslie dances to the strings.

It's better than I ever could have imagined. All the work this summer has strengthened Leslie's vocals, and despite the lack of time for mastery, she sounds solid. I'm mouthing the words along with her, once again conducting with my eyebrows.

She barely looks at me, her body twisting and turning, alternating between the classical ballet and the older, freer, dance of a different culture. This song represents that battle that's raging within her. Right now, she's not Leslie. She's Honor, letting go of the Dawn she crafted to meet the world's—and her family's—expectations. She is laying it all out on the line, making herself vulnerable, exposing her greatest weaknesses, for everyone to see.

By the time she finishes the number, triumphantly planting her feet and displaying a warrior posture in the middle of the stage, tears fill her eyes even as the breath rushes from her chest.

I sit there, unable to move, unable to speak.

"Huh." Tabitha's voice sounds so far away. What does that mean?

I stand up slowly. I should say something, but a coherent thought won't form. It's simply a swirl of emotions. I open my mouth when Leslie starts speaking.

Still taking deep breaths, gulping for air, she says, "Tabitha, don't judge Josh's brilliance on my performance. But I had to do this. For him. I had to let him know that I'm ready to accept my true self, even if it's not being the best. My true self does her best. My true self wants to give rather than take. And my true self will spend the rest of time trying to make it up to Josh for letting him down when he needed me most."

Before I know it, I'm crossing the room. I put my finger to her mouth, trying to stop her words. "Don't say anything else. I have to tell you something."

Leslie puts a shaking hand on mine, pulling it from her lips. She clenches it tightly, also grasping my other hand. "No, Josh, you have to hear me out. I wasn't there for you at the worst time in your life because I was too selfish to think about anything but my own misguided perceptions. I was about to let you down now too when you are standing on the cusp of greatness. I'm finally learning to love myself, and through that, I've realized how much I love you. I'd give anything to see your smile and to see you bite your lip and those adorable dancing eyebrows every single moment of every single day. You are the best thing that's ever happened to me. I need to start paying that back. If the best thing I ever do is help you succeed, then I'm going to do that. Every single day. Whatever it takes."

"Will you put that on a T-shirt?" I don't know why I say this, other than the mental image of Leslie in her family's T-shirt pops into my brain when she utters that saying.

Leslie nods. "Now what did you want to tell me?"

I smile. "In case you were wondering, I finally finished my show. I'm presenting it to Tabitha so she can see it before she finally invests."

Leslie shakes her head. "Oh really? What a surprise. It's about time you told me." She laughs. What a glorious sound.

"Oh my God, would you two kiss already?" Tabitha's voice rings out.

Leslie's head tips back in laughter. Don says, "I think that's another quote for the book."

Once Leslie's looking at me again, I take her jaw in my hand and say, "Tabitha's our boss now. If she says we should kiss, who are we to disappoint?" Leslie shakes her head slightly as I lean in. It's enough to make me pause, my own lips inches from hers. "No?"

Her breath hot on my mouth, she whispers, "I'm done doing what someone expects me to do. I can't live my life anymore for someone else's expectations. I have to do what's right for me."

Oh.

I start to pull back. As I do, Leslie throws her arms around my neck, pulling me in tight, kissing me with a hunger and passion that surprises me. Finally, she lightens the intensity. "And kissing you will always be what's right for me."

Epilogue

S o you're officially an actress now?" Meri's voice has the same level of enthusiasm it always does. As in *none*. She peers down at the playbill. "Leslie Layne. Doesn't have much character."

"But it's better than Moose. You know, an image that conjures up the dancing hippos from *Fantasia*."

Meri sinks back in the chair in my dressing room. "Oh God, you're right. I absolutely *loathe* the name. Sometimes I think Kaukauabulumakau would have been better."

I raise my eyebrow at her.

Finally, her hard veneer cracks and she laughs. "Oh, you're right. They're both terrible."

"But they're part of who we are. The strong fabric that weaves throughout our family and history and blood. But totally terrible names. Especially for a ballerina."

Except that's not how I identify anymore.

I'm so much more than that. I'm Leslie. I'm driven and passionate. I'm a good friend and a loving girlfriend. I'm a teacher and a teammate. I'm an actress and a dancer. I'm a sister and a daughter.

I'm not the best at any of them, but I do my best. There's a big difference.

"Okay, now shoo. I've got to get ready." As Meri stands, so do I. Awkwardly, I move to hug my big sister. She cocks her head. Right. We're not there yet. "Thanks for coming though. I appreciate you traveling all the way out here to see my show."

She shrugs. "Mom told me I had to."

I don't doubt it. "She is a force to be reckoned with."

"And she told me that Sergei from *Hollywood Dance Off!* would be here, and he's hot. I want you to introduce me to him."

"You watch that show?" I did not picture Dr. Meri Moose, Ph.D. to be the type to waste her time with such frivolity.

"Oh my God, yes. That and *The Bachelor*. I'm totally addicted. So can you hook me up?"

I have to laugh. She looks like a kid, asking her mom to get a candy bar at the checkout of the grocery store. "I can't hook you up because he's dating my boss's best friend, but I can introduce you to them all. I'm sure we can get some pics for social media at least."

Meri claps her hands and does a little jump. "This is totally worth it then." And she leaves.

I try not to read too much into it.

Josh comes walking into the dressing room. "You almost ready?"

I smile. "I was waiting until you came back before I put my lipstick on."

"Good call." He wraps his arms around me, pulling me tight to him. After he kisses me senseless, he says, "I still can't believe this is our life."

I know what he means. It's been a year since Five Boroughs Ballet Company released me from my contract. A year ago, I couldn't imagine a life without ballet.

I certainly didn't think I would ever be happy.

Yet this is more than I'd ever hoped for.

Kori and Mol haven't left for LA yet, though it's still in the works. I'm teaching at their studio, working around rehearsals for *Honor Code*, which Kori is of course choreographing. Brilliantly, I might add.

For the record, Josh didn't cast me because I was sleeping with him. Henderson was the one to make that decision. Mostly because Tabitha said to him, in no uncertain terms, and I quote, "If you let that badass ballerina slip through your hands one more time, I'll make you wish you'd never met me."

I'm so glad Henderson is able to live the drama-free life he's always dreamed about. For the record, that quote went in the book too.

Additionally, I would like to meme "badass ballerina."

I run my hands up Josh's arms, feeling his firm muscles underneath his black button-down shirt. "Have I ever told you how I love when you roll up your sleeves to show your forearms?" In reality, I love his sleeveless T-shirts even more, but he has to look professional while playing the piano in the pit.

Also, it's March in Upstate New York, so it's a balmy thirty-four degrees with an ice-cold rain out there. Once summer hits though, I'm confiscating all of his sleeved shirts.

He sits casually in the chair while I go about finishing my pre-show routine. I lean over the dressing table, applying my lipstick. I can feel his eyes on me. "What?" I smooth my hand over the backside of the pencil skirt I'm wearing for the opening number when I'm playing prim and proper Dawn.

"I wish my parents could be here to see this."

I turn to look at him. "They are. I'm sure of it." I walk over to him and sit down on his lap. I kiss him sweetly on the lips. "I shouldn't be kissing you. I already applied my lipstick. My routine is all messed up."

He kisses me again. "See? I knew all along you were a rule breaker."

"Rules like this are the best to break."

"There you go, using that 'b' word again."

"Break?" I feign innocence.

Josh kisses me lightly on the nose. "You know the one."

Best. The word that once hung like a weight around my neck—around my soul—now provides a buoyance to my life. One I didn't know even existed.

"It's hard not to use it. Not when I'm performing in the *best* show at the *best* theater with the *best* songs, and I get to come home to the *best* boyfriend who's the *best* lover I've ever had." I accentuate each *best* with a small kiss.

But it's true. When this all started, I didn't know who I was, let alone the best me. Josh and The Edison have helped the true Leslie shine through. I stand up, taking Josh's hand to lead him out to the pit.

My first love, my last love, my best love. We're going to succeed.

Whatever it takes.

The End

Acknowledgments

To Amy Basalusalu: Thank you for taking the time to talk to a total stranger about how wonder Fiji and its people are.

To Denise Lyle and Elle Rossi: Thank you for reading on behalf of your daughters. There's no one more protective than a momma, so I'm happy to have done you justice.

To Jake Goodman: Thank you for taking the time to answer my questions about all things singing and music for where my own Level 3 piano abilities left off.

To the Mac-Hadyn Theatre: Thank you for continuously being available, supportive, and nurturing with all my questions.

To the crew at Spendwood School of Dance and Gymnastics: Y'all know I'd be lost without you. You're my therapy.

To Heather Novak: Thank you for being such a vocal presence on social media that convinced me to watch *Julie and the Phantoms*. I wouldn't have a Josh without being inspired by Charlie Gillespie's adorable grin.

To Michele: This book is about Josh because of your dream. If I hit it big, you are *totally* organizing the party and are responsible for procuring all the Josh wine.

To Cahren: How many coincidences do we need for the stars to align and this book to make it big? I think we've had them all.

To my editors, Tami Lunch and Heather Balog: I can't thank you enough.

To my cat Butch, who felt this novel needed to be written with him laying on my arms: I'll be sending you the bill for my carpal tunnel. You're ridiculous.

About the Author

Armed with quick wit, relatable character, themes of resilience, and always a happy ending, award-winning and *USA Today* Bestselling author Kathryn R. Biel writes comfort reads. Balancing drama and angst with laughter and love, Kathryn weaves stories that will whisk you away for a few hours and have you rooting for the underdog, whether it's through sports romance, romantic comedy, or lighter women's fiction. By day, Kathryn is a pediatric physical therapist and Chief Domestic Officer of the Biel household. By night, when not writing, Kathryn can be found at the dance studio, knitting, watching sports with her husband and son, cuddling with her four cats, embarrassing herself on TikTok, and doing absolutely anything to avoid cleaning her house.

Kathryn is the author of 21 books, including the award-winning *Live for This*, *Made for Me*, and *The UnBRCAble Women Series (Ready for Whatever, Seize the Day,* and *Underneath It All)*.

Stand Alone Books:
Good Intentions
Hold Her Down
I'm Still Here
Jump, Jive, and Wail
Killing Me Softly
Live for This
Once in a Lifetime
Paradise by the Dashboard Light

Boston Buzzards:
XOXO
You Belong with Me
Zero to Hero

A New Beginnings Series:
Completions and Connections: A New Beginnings Novella
Made for Me
New Attitude
Queen of Hearts

The UnBRCAble Women Series:
Ready for Whatever
Seize the Day
Underneath It All

Center Stage Love Stories:
Act One: *Take a Chance on Me*
Act Two: *Vision of Love*
Act Three: *Whatever It Takes*

If you've enjoyed this book, please help the author out by leaving a review on **your** favorite retailer and **Goodreads.** A few minutes of your time makes a huge difference!

www.ingramcontent.com/pod-product-compliance
Lightning Source LLC
Chambersburg PA
CBHW031338020726
47499CB00005B/1325